THE POACHER
(An African Dilemma)

By
David Lemon

ISBN-13: 978-1530999644
ISBN-10: 1530999642

Cover design © Socciones

Design & formatting by Socciones Editoria Digitale

www.kindle-publishing-service.co.uk

Dedication

This is for six young citizens of Africa – **Gareth, Nicholas, Dale, Zara, Dougal and Kipling.** It is offered in the hope that you will love the wild places as much as I do.

Author's Note

Nata Pan National Park does not exist but many folk will recognise it as being an amalgamation of many of Zimbabwe's wonderful wild places. The characters in this story are also figments of my imagination, but a number of them featured in my very first book, Ivory Madness and it was a thrill to work with them again. The political incorrectness in this book is my fault, but bush life is never politically correct.

Although the story is totally imagined, as always I needed help with its construction. Lace sat through the original reading; Shelagh Brown brought my writing back to life with her quiet support and my Daughter in Law, Gillian Lemon helped with the vagaries of Australian slang. Thank you all. I could not have done it without you.

Contents

CHAPTER ONE
(Forced Landing)

She didn't have time to be frightened.

The Piper Commanche was easy to handle and Tracey Kemp tilted the aircraft into a smooth, banking turn at the outer end of her patrol. Below her, the Nata River twisted like a sluggish, silver python, its surface dotted and scarred by sand banks, tinged pink by the evening sun. Cloud shadows scudded across the landscape and behind her, the reflected cross of her aeroplane was highlighted by the sunset.

This was Tracey's kingdom - her home. This was the Nata Pan National Park - half a million hectares of unspoiled Africa and home to the largest variety of wild life to be found in the continent. As the park pilot, it was Tracey's task to fly over the entire area and check for possible problems at least twice a day. On a perfect November evening when late sunshine followed afternoon rain, it had to be the most wonderful job in the world and she knew that she was a very lucky young woman.

Setting the nose of the aircraft toward park headquarters at Nyamaketi, Tracey adjusted the trim and settled back to enjoy what remained of the evening patrol. She was looking forward to a quiet evening at home with Jason.

A family of bathing elephants flapped huge ears in desultory unconcern as she flashed overhead and further upstream, a herd of buffalo splashed through shallow water on their way to a heavily wooded island. From above, she could see the lurking shadows of monstrous crocodiles in the deeper water.

Dropping through three hundred metres of air space, Tracey kicked the rudder pedals and came around for another look at the buffalo. There must have been more than five hundred beasts in the water and her eyes glowed with appreciation of the moment.

Pulling the little half wheel back into her stomach, Tracey soared back into the evening sky, peering out through all sides of her perspex-enclosed cockpit. Away to her left, the Nata escarpment glowed a deep, burnished orange in the fading light, dark shadows across its face showing where rain still fell. Closer to hand, but still south of the river, the Makorokoro was already in deep shadow and Tracey suppressed an almost superstitious shiver of unease. She loved the park and enjoyed every moment spent in its wild surroundings, but she was terrified of the Makorokoro.

Home to vast herds of elephant and the few black rhinoceros left in the valley, this was a dark, brooding area of dense forest with a history of violent death and destruction. Once the rains were under way, it was cut off from the rest of the park, the only access road, a slippery quagmire of evil red mud.

Looking down on the dark carpet of trees, Tracey wondered what was happening beneath that tangled covering. There would undoubtedly be poachers at work, hunting the great, grey elephants and ever scarcer rhinoceros - gunning them down with automatic weapons and perhaps being gunned down in turn by Security Force units. There was a war going on in the Makorokoro and government patrols had orders to shoot poachers on sight.

Poaching for the pot had long been a tradition among people of the Nata Valley and their activities had usually been overlooked by the authorities as doing no lasting damage to the environment. That state of affairs had ended with the advent of automatic weaponry and the imposition by CITES in 1988 of a worldwide ban on trade in ivory. Demand for the precious substance had grown in the Far East and prices on the illegal market had rocketed. Now that the elephant and rhinoceros populations had been decimated in countries north of the river, a new breed of poacher had appeared in the park. Armed with high-powered Kalashnikovs, these men ruthlessly butchered the animals and the situation had degenerated into a bitter conflict between poachers and the forces of law and order.

Men on both sides had died and Tracey shivered again as she turned her attention to the landscape beyond the northern bank of the river.

This was another vast area of rugged countryside, uninhabited except for a handful of tiny villages huddling on the edge of the Nata. Behind these scattered dwellings, great, sweeping swathes of rocky hillside drifted inland to distant horizons. It was an awe inspiring vista that never failed to thrill and make Tracey proud to be part of this greatest of continents. Africa was her home, yet she could never get enough of it.

Tracey was idly watching a dug out canoe on the river when the engine cut out. There was no warning; no preparatory stutter or cough - it just died. One moment, the big 250 horse power Lycoming motor thrummed reassuringly in front of her, the propeller, a shimmering blur of speed. The next, she was surrounded by whistling wind and the fluted blade revolved with sluggish mockery in front of the windscreen. Her stomach lurched nervously as she dropped toward inevitable disaster in the gathering darkness.

Below the helpless aircraft, the Nata Valley still looked spectacularly beautiful. The river still gleamed a deep, burnished bronze, while Mopani forest spread in a purple carpet across the valley floor and the setting sun bespattered the sky with a kaleidoscope of colour. Tracey no longer noticed the magnificence of her home. Hours of dedicated training came into immediate effect and professional pilot took the place of enthusiastic young woman.

Her immediate task was to convert forward speed into extra height, thereby allowing herself more time for manoeuvre. The wind was coming from directly behind her and pulling the control wheel gently backwards once again, Tracey watched the nose lift toward the heavens. For nearly eight seconds, the crippled Piper climbed, levelling off with the altimeter showing just over seven hundred metres. Her fingers drumming nervously on one knee, Tracey rapidly calculated how long she had to get herself out of trouble.

Without power, the aircraft would lose height at two hundred metres a minute, so she had roughly three and a half minutes to play with - not a great deal of time when her life was at stake.

Casting that gloomy thought from her mind, Tracey looked around for somewhere to land. In a normal glide without power from that height, she could travel about six thousand metres in a straight line, but the landscape below her was darkly forbidding. The Makorokoro on one side of the river and those gaunt, craggy hills on the other. Neither option appealed. What few forest clearings, she could see were broken up with baobab trees or were far too small to land in with any degree of safety. This was the most thickly forested area of the park and to bring the crippled Piper down among the trees was a recipe for certain death.

The river provided a possible alternative and Tracey studied it doubtfully. Curving into the western horizon, it gleamed like beaten pewter in the waning light, but wide sandbanks carved the water apart and nowhere could she see an area that offered sufficient space for a forced landing.

Nearly ten kilometres ahead, a strange yellow hill offered momentary hope. Jutting like a rotten pimple from the valley floor, it was known as Tombekule and Tracey knew that it was surrounded by wide mud flats. However it was probably well out of range for her stricken aircraft and landing on soft mud would he risky. Rolling the Piper to the left, Tracey scanned the nearer countryside with mounting anxiety. Time was running out fast.

Close to the foot of the escarpment, water flashed among the trees and she turned somewhat reluctantly toward this momentary offer of hope. Makorokoro Pan was a dangerously inhospitable spot, but it was nearly three hundred and fifty metres long, so it did at least give her a chance to bring the Piper down. A belly landing on water was always a risky business, especially in near darkness, but Tracey no longer had any alternative. Taking a deep breath, she fingered the carved ivory figurine at her throat and prayed for a little luck. With the tail wind and the Piper at its lightest, she might just make it.

Thinking furiously and making a conscious effort to remain calm, Tracey worked out her plan of action. Now that she was committed to landing on the pan, she trimmed the elevators and ran her eyes anxiously across the banked dials and instruments at her fingertips. Temperature and oil pressure gauges read normal; both fuel tanks were half full; the fuel pump was apparently working, the mixture control set to 'rich' and the primer was locked. If the problem lay with fuel or the lubrication system, it was not readily apparent. It had to be something to do with the aircraft electrics.

Running tense fingers across the controls, Tracey checked the ignition switch. Engine current was provided by two magnetos and she moved the switch across to them both. Left - that was okay; right - no problem. The switch covering both magnetos, she brought the electric starter into play. It was her last chance.

With a spluttering cough, the engine turned asthmatically over, but there was no sign of life. The propeller spun uselessly and Tracey chewed anxiously on her lower lip. Whatever the problem was, the engine was not going to start and she knew with sick certainty in her stomach that a forced landing was inevitable.

Although she had been flying for five years and was one of the most experienced pilots in the department, Tracey had never put an aircraft down without power and looking out at the landscape below, she knew that she could not have chosen a less hospitable spot. Tears of anxious frustration sprang to her eyes and she wondered what Jason Willard would have done in her predicament. How she longed for the big man's comforting presence beside her. How she longed for the gentle rumble of his voice and the feel of his strong arms around her in this moment of crisis.

But Jason would not even be aware of the danger she was facing. She had to put park headquarters in the picture. Looking anxiously around her and wondering what else she might have forgotten, Tracey reached for the VHF radio, fixed to the control panel. Striving to keep her voice level, she pressed the 'transmit' button.

"Nata, Nata - this is Skybird. I've got a 'mayday' - over."

The operator at Nyamaketi cut in immediately.

"What is the problem, Skybird - over?"

"I have an in-flight emergency and want the warden urgently - over."

"Stand by, Skybird."

The operator had caught the tension in her voice and she could imagine him running into the corridor at Nyamaketi and shouting for the warden. Smiling tightly at the mental picture, she reflected on the incongruity of office routine going on while she faced the possibility of a nasty death less than twenty minutes flying time away from where they were working. For all that, the prospect of hearing Jason's deep voice on the set immediately eased her nervousness. He might not be able to bring the aircraft down for her, but he would at least provide emotional support and comfort through the trying moments ahead.

Lightning tore raggedly across the western horizon and the radio screeched with atmospheric noises. Tracey adjusted the tuning knob, but crackling static drowned out everything else. She was vaguely aware of a voice on the set, but in spite of her frenzied fine tuning, she could not make out individual words.

With mounting anxiety, she checked her instruments again. The Piper was dropping with alarming rapidity and she would soon be too low for satisfactory radio communication in any case. This was a notoriously difficult area for reception and she didn't have much time.

"I'm in trouble, Nata." She spoke urgently into the microphone. "I've lost all power and am coming down in the Makorokoro. I will try to land on the pan itself - over."

The set screeched an eerie acknowledgement and she wondered if anyone had heard the message. Feeling suddenly lonely and afraid, she replaced the handset in its cradle with helpless tears threatening to overwhelm her.

Another hundred metres of precious air space had been used up when she heard the calm tones of the Nata Research Officer, Jim Lewis. His transmission was spasmodic and interspersed with screeching static, but it helped to steady her nerves. At least she was not entirely alone.

"...... strength two, My Girl. I'll try for....... Air Force...... but.... get a truck..... here..... a rough night, but

7

they will.... as soon as...."

The ecologist's final words were lost in crackling atmospherics and Tracey was too involved in her own immediate troubles to acknowledge. As long as they knew where she was, rescue was someone else's problem and she concentrated on flying the crippled Piper.

The world was very dark below the aeroplane, but the water of Makorokoro pan showed clearly through the gathering gloom. She would only have one chance, so she had to get the landing right. She would need to approach from the far end of the pan to face whatever prevailing wind there might be at ground level. Hopefully, she would touch down on the water with space to spare on both sides and come to rest near the northern shore. The pan was notorious for the size of its resident crocodiles and Tracey had no wish to swim, particularly as she would almost certainly be spending the night out in the open. Wet clothing would make things even more uncomfortable.

As she banked the aircraft, the rate of descent increased alarmingly and Tracey's hands tightened involuntarily on the control wheel. She was still a long way out and every metre of height was precious. The slowly milling propeller was creating extra drag and as the aircraft slowed, so it dropped more quickly. She had to increase her speed, but that meant putting the nose down and if her calculations were wrong, she wasn't going to make the pan.

With her mouth suddenly dry and doubts crowding her mind, Tracey deliberately lowered the nose and watched anxiously as the air speed indicator began to move. Eighty knots became ninety, then a hundred - one hundred and ten. As the aircraft sliced through the evening, she was suddenly aware of wind whistling eerily around the cockpit. It was in sharp contrast to the normal sounds of flying and the comparative silence made Tracey even more aware of her own vulnerability in the tiny perspex cocoon. Desperately closing her mind to fear, she levelled out the glide path and concentrated on her landing.

One hundred and sixty metres above the ground, she pulled on a small handle and sections of the wing moved downward, steadying the aeroplane and reducing the speed once more. The Piper dropped ever more rapidly and as the pan showed to her left, Tracey prayed that there would be no basking hippopotami or sunken trees in the area, she had chosen for her landing.

The water looked black, flat and empty, but her stomach was knotted with anxiety as she banked for the final turn. Steadying the aircraft with the wheel and rudder pedals, she felt for her ivory talisman and looked up to the heavens for luck.

With level flight, her speed was dropping fast again and she watched it carefully. A stall at this juncture would be disastrous and almost certainly fatal. The altimeter showed forty metres and there could be no recovery from that height. Eighty knots; seventy knots; sixty five - the pan opened up in front of her, a wide expanse of dark, uninviting water. Absently, she wondered whether it would be cold and giggled nervously at the thought.

Breathing deeply to control her fluttering nerves, Tracey applied full flaps and turned off the master switch, thereby shutting down all power in the aircraft. She was vaguely aware of a hippo pod looking up in startled surprise as she rushed over their heads, then she made a last, deliberate effort to relax her panic-stricken grip on the control wheel.

With her eyes on the dark water hurtling past, Tracey Kemp lifted the nose of the aircraft and braced herself for the coming impact.

There was nothing more, she could do.

*   *   *

"Where is the warden, Man?"

Jim Lewis shouted the question at the office orderly and that young man shrugged his shoulders.

"He went out in his Land Rover, Sir. He did not tell me where he was going and he has not booked out in the diary."

Lewis grunted angrily. It was accepted practice than anyone leaving camp should enter their destination in the office diary and it was a practice that had been initiated by Willard himself. That the park warden chose to ignore his own instructions was out of character, but it was too late to worry about it. Struggling to disguise his concern, Lewis concentrated on organising rescue for Tracey Kemp.

In spite of his reassuring tones on the radio, the bearded ecologist was sick with worry. Due to the appalling reception, he had not been able to verify the site of Tracey's intended landing and he studied the map on the wall of the radio room with a grim frown. Wherever she came down, her chances of survival were minimal, but if she had chosen the Makorokoro, they were reduced to the wildly improbable.

She had mentioned the pan and that was a place that Lewis knew well. It lay in wild, inhospitable countryside, infested with lions and other dangerous animals. Makorokoro Pan was not a nice place to spend the night in the best of circumstances and any overland rescue attempt would encounter enormous difficulties. With the rains well under way, road conditions would be appalling and even with luck on their side, it could take days to locate the crashed aircraft if it had come down anywhere close to the pan.

By then, it would almost certainly be far too late.

Seething with angry nervousness, Lewis puffed on a large pipe while he adjusted dials on the big, short-wave radio. A few minutes later, he was speaking to a wing commander at Seven Squadron Headquarters – the home of the Air Force helicopters. The airman was sympathetic, but could offer no immediate assistance.

"We can't get a chopper there before tomorrow evening, Jim." He told the Parks man. "I know that is small comfort to your pilot, but we have three aircraft in dock and a big anti poaching operation going on up in...."

"That's okay, Gideon," Lewis cut him off. "I'll send a party overland tonight and hopefully, they will find her at the pan. It is the only place in the Makorokoro where she stands any chance of coming down in one piece. Mind you, it is raining steadily now, so it will be one hell of a job.

'Anyway, I will come back to you as soon as I have anything definite."

"Good man." The airman was matter of fact about such things. He had seen all too many forced landings and crashes in his time. "I will put Air Traffic Control in the picture and they will doubtless send crash investigators up once you have located the aircraft."

"They should be a great help," Lewis commented with bitter sarcasm and the wing commander chuckled sympathetically.

"Don't mind me, Gideon," Jim Lewis went on grimly. "I am a little upset, but we will find her somehow."

Carefully replacing the microphone, Lewis momentarily buried his face in his hands. He was a vastly experienced scientist, but this was a situation, he was not trained to face. He had worked with Tracey Kemp for a long time and she was his friend as well as a valued colleague. Now she was in desperate trouble and he had no way of helping her. She could be in pain; she could

11

even be dead. He glanced automatically at his watch. By now, she would definitely be down and the rain outside was getting harder. Jim Lewis wondered what to do next.

His gloomy reverie was interrupted by the noisy arrival in the radio room of rangers, Willie Sibanda and Mark Nicholson, two large young men who had run across from their own quarters to find out what was going on. Dispassionately, Lewis explained the situation and his own doubts as to what could be done.

"Bloody hell!" Sibanda frowned at the map on the wall. "We will struggle to reach the Makorokoro in this rain."

"What about the army?" Nicholson asked. "They might have patrols in that area who could assist."

Lewis nodded absently.

"I will get on to their HQ, but in the meantime, we have to do something ourselves. You guys get yourselves prepared for a rescue mission. Take a couple of scouts, a stretcher and full first aid kit, including saline drips. If Tracey did come down on the pan, there is a good chance of finding her alive, but she will be pretty knocked about. If this rain doesn't get any worse, you might be lucky enough to get within a few kilometres of the crash site and if you go hard, you could have her found and patched up before mid morning."

"And if she came down somewhere else?"

It was Sibanda who put the question and Lewis looked bleak.

"Then she is almost certainly dead."

The dreadful word seemed to linger on in the room long after he had said it and both rangers looked shocked at the thought of their colleague's plight. It was almost as though they hadn't considered the possibility. Lewis knew that he was asking a great deal of the two young men. They were both very fond of Tracey so the search would be deeply personal, but he had nobody else to turn to. Trying to keep his worries off his face, he went on in a gentler tone.

"If you cannot find her at or near the pan, just stay put until we can get the choppers in there. By then it will definitely be too late, but in the meantime I will alert any army and police patrols in the Makorokoro. We might just get lucky and have one close at hand."

But even that was to be no easy task. Lewis informed Police General Headquarters about the missing aircraft, only to be told that Support Unit patrols in the area were out of contact for the night. Army headquarters were even less forthcoming.

"I don't think we have anyone in the Makorokoro." The duty officer sounded disinterested. "If we do, I will ensure that they are informed of the situation, first thing in the morning."

"I don't suppose the fool even knows where the Makorokoro is," Lewis fumed as he slammed down the radio telephone receiver then shook his head in weary frustration. With the warden's absence, he had to take charge of the situation, but he neither enjoyed nor wanted the responsibility. He took his frustration out on the radio operator.

"Don't just sit there, Man. Keep trying to raise 'Skybird.' She might be able to hear us and a friendly voice can only be a comfort if she is down in somewhere like the Makorokoro.

'Keep trying for the warden as well. He should be here, not gallivanting around in the ruddy bush."

While the two young rangers prepared themselves for an almost impossible rescue attempt, Jim Lewis could only wait, hope and pray.

CHAPTER TWO
(Makorokoro Pan)

The aeroplane seemed to be travelling impossibly fast.

As dark water rushed up to meet her, Tracey was dimly aware of skeletal trees flashing past the windows. Casting a final, automatic glance across the instrument panel, she was vaguely surprised to see that her ground speed was fifty five knots - exactly right for a forced landing on water.

With her hands feather-light on the controls and her mind racing over those aspects of the landing that had to be considered, Tracey brought the Piper down exactly one hundred and twenty metres from the northern shore. As she raised the nose and levelled out only centimetres above the water, she touched the lucky figurine around her throat and breathing a silent prayer to the God of distressed aviators, concentrated on holding the hurtling aeroplane as straight and level as she could.

She felt the whispered touch as the belly of the fuselage sliced through tiny wavelets and for a few seconds, she wondered if that was all there was to it. Spray fountained around the cockpit and sheets of murky water cascaded down the windscreen and then she felt the first shattering impact and the Piper bounced off the surface of the pan like a rubber ball on concrete. The safety harness dug agonisingly into her shoulders and she was hurled violently forward.

Desperately trying to hold the madly kicking control wheel, Tracey felt as though she was caught up in the bowels of a wildly gyrating cement mixer. The aeroplane bounced twice more before digging its belly into the water and the dark shoreline seemed to hurtle towards her with ever increasing speed.

The Piper was an old aircraft and although it had been

beautifully made, two retaining pins in the seat assembly sheered off in the initial impact. The seat swivelled violently, Tracey's right leg smashed sickeningly into the bottom edge of the control panel and she screamed aloud with the sheer agony of the moment. A loose fire extinguisher smashed into her ribs and her head crashed against a side window. Pain battered at her senses from all angles and she was only vaguely conscious as the aircraft careered in a fountain of spray toward the hard and unyielding shore.

As forward momentum slowed, one wing tip dipped and bit deep into the water. The Piper slewed violently and in spite of her harness, Tracey's head bounced heavily off the forward windscreen. Vivid flashes of white light seared through her vision and she felt hot vomit surge in the back of her throat.

The crashing noises of impact built up into a roaring crescendo and then - as suddenly as it had started - the noise died away and Tracey found herself in a softly floating cocoon of semi consciousness. Her world was dreamily silent, apart from the gentle splash of water running down the fuselage and an insistent drumming sensation inside her head.

Slowly, blearily, Tracey Kemp returned to full consciousness and with awareness, came a sudden flare of panic. Every pilot lives with the fear of fire and Tracey was no exception. Frantically, she checked that all switches were in the 'off' position and reached for the door handle.

The movement brought pain searing through her leg and she couldn't help a gasping cry of torment. Taking deep breaths to steady her nerves, she made a conscious effort to remain calm.

The Piper had carved its way through a long stretch of relatively calm water, so the dangers of fire were minimal.

She was not sure whether she was afloat or resting on land, so it would be foolish to leap out of the door without sizing up the situation. Automatically checking the control panel for the last time, Tracey slid the side window open and peered into the evening. The aircraft had come to rest in shallow water, but with a sense of relief, she saw that it was solidly aground. One wing was submerged, but it was only a small step from the aeroplane on to dry land. She would not have to swim and for the moment, any lurking crocodiles would have been scared away by the noises of impact. Moving carefully out of her seat, she bit back another cry of anguish as pain ripped through her body again.

Her right leg was jammed awkwardly beneath the instrument panel and blood matted the front of her flying overalls. Every movement brought fresh torment lancing through her body and she guessed that the leg was probably broken. Forcing herself to remain calm, Tracey considered her position.

She could not stay in the aircraft - that was obvious. Quite apart from the fire risk, it would leave her trapped and vulnerable to any emergency. The Makorokoro was a favourite haunt of poachers and they would not be kindly disposed to any game ranger they chanced upon, even if she was badly hurt.

Quite apart from the risk involved, the damaged cockpit was claustrophobic and she needed fresh air. She had to get out. Moving slowly and deliberately, Tracey eased the injured limb out from under the instrument panel with both hands and carefully opened the door.

Darkness had fallen and the night was desperately quiet - the bush inhabitants shocked into silence by the horrific noise of the crash. It was but a short step from the cockpit to the wing and an even shorter one from there, but for Tracey, they were almost insurmountable. With both hands gripping her injured leg, she manoeuvred herself slowly on to the wing, paused on one leg to catch her breath then fell with a shuddering crash into shallow water. Her leg smashed against solid ground and the pain made her entire body convulse in dreadful agony.

Tracey Kemp was a very strong young lady, both mentally and physically. She held down a job that was too much for many men and she was accustomed to the discomfort of spartan bush patrols. But this was more than mere discomfort. Pain of incredible intensity rushed through her body to smash against her brain in a blinding flash of viciously white light.

Throwing back her head, Tracey screamed her agony to the darkness. Wavelets washed soothingly against her face and blood ran from her leg to infuse with dark water. Above her prostrate body, the night sky came slowly to life and frogs resumed their interrupted chorus. Tracey noticed none of it. Merciful oblivion had moved in to counter the pain and she was deeply unconscious.

**

"Warden, Warden, Warden - this is Nata - do you read me - over?"

The radio remained silent and Jim Lewis muttered angrily as he replaced the handset. It was three hours since Tracey's 'mayday' message and deep lines of strain were showing on the ecologist's face.

"Where is the bloody bloke - he should be here?" He muttered to Willie Sibanda, but the younger man merely shook his head. The ranger had his rescue party ready to move out, but their Land Cruiser was giving trouble and Mark Nicholson was making last minute repairs.

"Probably broken down somewhere," Sibanda grunted laconically. "All our transport is in such a ruddy mess, it's a wonder we ever get anywhere."

"Jason has been a little down of late," Lewis mused. "I reckon the forthcoming cull is worrying him. I taxed him about it the other day, but you know what he is like. Just told me that I was imagining things.

'The trouble is, I've got to put Headquarters in the picture about Tracey and they are going to ask why I'm running the show instead of the warden."

Sibanda laughed coarsely.

"The silly buggers probably won't even notice, Jim. Those bloody desk jockeys haven't a clue what goes on in places like this and besides, you'll be lucky to find anyone in Head Office at this time of night."

"That's true, but I'll have to get through soon or we'll be in trouble when the company opens up in the morning."

With obvious reluctance, he reached for the radio telephone, glancing up momentarily at the arrival of Mark Nicholson. The burly ranger was dressed in camouflage overalls and carried a heavy rifle. His hands were covered in grease and water dripped down his face as he threw himself into a chair.

"I'll have that heap sorted out in another twenty minutes." Nicholson mopped his face with a large handkerchief. "In the meantime, it is raining buckets out there. We won't even be able to start out in this, let alone reach Makorokoro.

'Tracey picked one hell of a night to fall out of the sky."

"That is all we bloody well need." Lewis scowled helplessly at the radio, but the set remained obstinately silent and with a shrug of resignation, Jim Lewis started to dial.

Water in her mouth and throbbing agony in her leg brought Tracey gasping to the surface of consciousness. For a moment, she wondered where she was, then memory flooded back and she raised her head to look around her with clouded eyes. Her teeth chattered with shock and she felt the deep lassitude of despair envelop her being. In the distance, a hyena howled and her scalp crawled with anxiety. Her leg felt as though it was swollen to three times its normal size and as she moved, fresh agony erupted in her thigh, bringing tears to her eyes and making her sob with frightened frustration.

Gulping with the effort, Tracey struggled to keep herself from weeping. She could imagine what Jason Willard would say - could see the mocking glint in his eye as he said it.

"Come on, my Chicken; pull yourself together. The pain is not real. You only think you're hurting."

How often had she heard those or similar words as he urged her to greater endeavour in the past? The memory of his gentle mockery made her sniffle again and she made a determined effort to pull herself together. Moving her body around, she gripped the injured leg with both hands and tried to pull it with her so that she could roll on to dry land. The movement brought vomit to her mouth and she whimpered aloud. Blood oozed over her hands and she stopped suddenly, unsure how to go on. She was stuck uncomfortably in the shallows, unable to go forward or back without incurring further agony. Behind her, water stretched black and uninviting, while on the shoreline in front, huge, dark shadows looked terribly menacing. Tracey knew that she was in desperate trouble.

Unable to help herself, she burst into tears at the thought that she might even be dying, injured and alone in the dark Makorokoro. For nearly two minutes, she wept before making a determined effort to pull herself together. Stifling her sobs, she forced herself to smile through her tears and cursed herself for a snivelling cry baby.

"You are a big girl now, Tracey Kemp." She told herself sternly. "Now act like one and stop this silly blubbering."

But in spite of the brave words, she felt desperately alone and frightened. She wanted her Jason. She needed his comforting presence beside her; longed for his strong arms and soothing kisses. In her mind, she could hear his deep voice murmuring encouragement and comfort.

But Jason was not beside her and whatever happened, she knew there were many hours of painful suffering and discomfort to endure before he arrived. Lowering her head on to the mud, Tracey closed her eyes, but even as she drifted into fitful sleep, a fresh wave of pain slammed through her leg.

Stifling a shriek, she reached for the talisman around her neck, but her fingers found only smooth, bare skin. The figurine - her good luck charm for so many years - had disappeared in the crash and for a moment, she felt a deep stab of premonitory fear. All pilots are notoriously superstitious and Tracey was no exception. Without her lucky talisman, she knew she could not possibly survive the long night ahead, particularly as the figurine had been a gift from Jason. He had presented it to her on the occasion of her first solo flight and urged her to wear it whenever she took to the air.

"It will keep you safe in the worst of times, Little Chicken." He had rumbled lovingly and since that memorable day, the talisman had never left her neck. Now it was gone and she felt a deep sense of foreboding. Tears welled up again as she thought about the figurine.

Delicately carved from a single piece of ivory, it

depicted the mythical snake God of the Nata Valley - a Spirit both benevolent and generous toward those who sought its help. Jason had originally taken the carving from Simeon - arguably the most notorious poacher in the history of the Parks Department, but a veritable artist with his whittling knife.

Now the carving had gone and without it, Tracey felt terribly vulnerable and close to despair. She moaned fretfully into the darkness and from the edge of the forest, cold topaz eyes blinked at the unhappy sound.

***

The radio room at Nyamaketi was filled with smoke from Lewis' pipe and a succession of cigarettes, smoked by Willie Sibanda. Outside, the camp generator thumped rhythmically into the darkness and the lights were clouded by frantically circling insects. Distant thunder seemed to accentuate the tension in the room.

Nicholson and two scouts sat mutely in one corner, while Lewis had his feet on the radio table and Sibanda paced fretfully around the room. Only the radio operator seemed unaffected by the gravity of the situation. He concentrated on a torn and crumpled copy of an old magazine, he had rescued from the waste basket, but even he kept half his mind on Lewis, waiting for the research officer to flare up again. All of them raised their heads at the rumbling swish made by an approaching vehicle and it was Willie Sibanda who ran into the corridor to peer out into driving rain.

"It is the warden." He called over his shoulder as he recognised Land Rover headlights.

"Thank God for that."

Lewis swung his feet down from the table as Jason Willard dripped his way into the room.

"What on earth are you lot doing here at this time of night?" The warden's tone reflected concerned astonishment. "It is well after ten and getting wetter by the minute."

"Waiting for you." Lewis told him shortly. "Tracey has gone down somewhere in the Makorokoro."

There was no gentle way of imparting the news and Willard stopped in mid stride. It was almost as though he had walked into a wall and his face reflected careful control of his feelings as he turned to the ecologist. To have any member of his staff in danger was bad enough, but with Tracey involved, Lewis' softly spoken words had hit him particularly hard.

Quietly and with a minimum of emotion, Lewis recounted the story as he knew it.

"The lads would have been half way there by now," he finished off, "but as usual, we've had vehicle problems and just as Mark got the bloody truck going, this downpour set in. I reckon we will just have to sit it out."

His tone was vaguely defensive and there were a few moments of silence in the room as Willard struggled to take in the news. An experienced pilot himself, he knew only too well the problems involved in a forced landing on the valley floor. In the Makorokoro, those problems would be amplified threefold. The fact that Tracey was the pilot involved made an already desperate situation into something of a nightmare and he struggled to remain calm. Tracey Kemp was more than just a member of his staff. She was his life and his reason for being. Jason Willard's heart burned at the thought of her lying injured and afraid in that dark and terrible corner of the park. Getting her out would be enormously difficult, but the warden was a resourceful man and resolved that he would walk in and carry her out if he had to.

Pulling himself together with an obvious effort, he

22

strode across to the wall map and studied it carefully.

"You're right, Jim," he said softly. "It has to be the pan. The only other spot that looks flat is the land around Tombekule, but that is terribly muddy and Tracey is too good a pilot to risk a forced landing in that stuff. I hope she is at any rate."

There was almost a whimper in the big man's voice as he said the last few words, then he braced himself once more and turned to the rangers.

"I want you guys on the road as soon as possible." he ordered briskly. "Make for the pan and never mind the rain. It is not going to let up now. Just be sure your winch is working and take plenty of shovels and buck boards. Go nice and easy through the bad spots, Willie and you should do it in seven hours or so.

'Off you go then."

The rangers and their men were half way to the door when Lewis spoke up. He had been frowning heavily over his pipe as Willard issued his instructions and now he shook his head in muted objection.

"Hold on Jason; let's not go off half cocked for God's sake. We only have the Land Cruiser and your truck working, so if Tracey is not at the pan, we are going to have one hell of a search on our hands. We only need one vehicle stuck in the mud and the whole op will grind to a halt. Then where will we be?"

Willard turned to look at him, uncertainty showing plainly on his craggy features. The two rangers stood in silence, waiting for the senior men to come to a decision.

"I can understand your impatience to get going, "Lewis went on quietly, "but we have to do things systematically or Tracey won't stand a chance. Face it, Jason; if we mess this one up, your girl is going to die."

Once again, Lewis' blunt way of expressing the facts

brought silence to the room. Willard rubbed one hand helplessly across his jaw and the sound of rasping stubble was almost deafening.

"Yes of course - you're right, Jim." He sounded almost pathetic in his confusion. "Hold on you guys and let's wait for the rain to ease up a bit."

Bracing his shoulders with an obvious effort, the warden turned back to Lewis.

"Get back on to headquarters, Jim and have a word with the regional warden. If that rhino relocation exercise is still going on at Chimanga, I want authority to hire their helicopter. It will cost a bomb, but this is a bloody emergency, so they just have to cough up."

Lewis momentarily chided himself for forgetting the Chimanga exercise, although he wasn't sure that he would have had the gall to ask for a chopper in any case. They had only recently received yet more instructions for financial cutbacks in the department and the rhino relocation operation was privately funded. Hiring their chopper could take a great deal of explaining, even for the regional warden.

"Their little chopper won't be much good for a rescue attempt, Jason," he muttered doubtfully. "Have you seen the ruddy thing? There's no room for anyone but the pilot."

"Of course I have seen it, Man. We'll make room if we have to damnit!" Having already conceded one point, Willard was anxious to reassert his authority. "We can at least get someone in there to see if Tracey's okay. She is going to need medical attention and I can't see us getting in by road before noon, even if everything goes well."

It took another twenty minutes to raise the base camp at Chimanga, but at last the frustrated warden was speaking to a disembodied, American voice. The man on the other end was instantly sympathetic however and promised to have a pilot at Nyamaketi by first light.

"You might find him a bit of a weird character;" He warned Willard; "but there is no better bush pilot about. If anyone can get your girl out of there, Aussie Jack Meadows is the man."

"I don't care if he has five legs and a stutter, as long as he can ruddy well fly."

Jason Willard looked a troubled man as he replaced the radio handset.

***

With her cheek resting on wet sand and her injured leg stretched awkwardly behind her, Tracey listened with a sense of deep foreboding to the noises of the night. She felt terribly vulnerable where she lay, but the effort involved in moving, effectively precluded any further action – at least for the moment. As she listened, she wondered what to do.

A few hundred metres away, another hyena cackled spitefully, to be answered from the opposite side of the pan. Tracey could not control the sudden shiver of fear that ran down her spine. Hyenas were not nice beasts to have around when one was bleeding and helpless in the bush. She prayed that they would leave her alone.

Closing her eyes against the unfriendly night, she made a determined effort to forget about the painful discomfort of her injury and allowed her mind to drift into anguished daydreams. Most of them centred around Jason Willard. How she loved that man.

Tracey had been a teenager when her class at school had been addressed by a craggy young ranger from the Parks Department. He had made an immediate impression and the ecological problems of Africa became her focus in life.

It had come as no surprise to anyone who knew her when Tracey had chosen to study the subject at university. It was there that she met up with Jason Willard again. The big man had been studying for a zoology degree and their unexpected meeting marked the start of the most enjoyable period of her life.

Jason Willard was still a game ranger and while at the university was based in a small park less than fifteen kilometres from the city boundary. Although she was considerably younger than he was, Tracey Kemp had attracted him from the start. A pretty, vivacious girl, he was captivated by her beaming enthusiasm for life and the way her face seemed to light up when he mentioned wild life or the bush. At first, they merely talked together and shared knowledge when it came to revision, but it wasn't long before their relationship deepened and Willard began taking her out on weekends.

It seemed natural to spend their time together in the park where Willard worked and it was there that he gave Tracey her first practical lessons in what was to become her life's work. They walked for hours through the bush, creeping up on unsuspecting animals so that Willard could point out how to differentiate between species and genders. They camped out at night and he showed her the stars, explaining the various constellations and their place in the universal order of life. He showed her wild beasts in their natural habitat and explained the attributes of trees and the uses to which they could be put. Tracey was a quick learner and soon began surprising her unofficial tutor with her aptitude for the path she had chosen. To his delight, she flourished in adverse conditions and excelled in obscure occupations such as tracking and finding water in the dry places.

It wasn't long before Jason Willard had taken over Tracey's entire existence. She found herself deeply in love and the big man was everything to her – teacher, older brother and gently expert lover. He was as delighted as she was when their results came out and she had passed with flying colours. As a direct result of his own new degree, he was promoted to the rank of game warden and they celebrated their joint success with great good humour. A qualified pilot himself, Willard had bought her flying lessons as a birthday present and she had proved a natural in the air, gaining her PPL within six months of the initial lesson.

Armed with a first class honours degree and a private pilot's license, Tracey could have chosen almost any well-paying path in life, but Jason Willard encouraged her to apply for a post with the Air Wing of the Parks Department. Not only had she been accepted, but she had been posted straight to the great park at Nata Pan, where Willard himself had been transferred as the warden in charge. Although she had never dared to ask, it seemed likely that he had exerted some influence somewhere.

Tracey's first two years at Nata Pan were undoubtedly the best years of her life. Quite apart from the opportunity to work with the man she admired most in the world, she loved being among the animals and birds of her vast, new home. She enjoyed the close companionship and camaraderie of the bush people and she loved the hours, spent flying over her kingdom. Occasionally, she was called away to other parks in order to assist with counting or culling operations, but in the main, her time was spent at Nata Pan. She loved her life with the man who had made it all possible and the only minor blight on her happiness was that Jason showed no inclination to get married. She knew that he loved her as much as she loved him, but something made him shy away from total commitment and that she found difficult to understand.

Apart from that, her life at Nata Pan was an idyllic one. In time, she would study for a Masters degree, but for the moment, she was content.

Now it seemed that it was all about to come to an end and Tracey wondered how Willard would be coping with news of her forced landing. She knew he would be frantic with worry and in spite of her own pain and anxiety, she wished there was some way of reassuring him. Surely he deserved better than to worry himself sick over her. With a groan of frustrated despair, Tracey shook her head to banish another sudden flood of tears.

Dimly seen in the gloom, an elephant wandered down to drink only thirty metres away, but she was not alarmed. Jason had taught her about elephants and she knew that they were the kindest, most gentle creatures on earth. If she was in any danger, it certainly would not come from elephants.

Watched by more curious eyes from the trees, Tracey Kemp cradled her head on one arm and tried to sleep.

CHAPTER THREE
(The Poacher)

Deep in a tangled thicket, the poacher watched nervously. As daylight faded in the West, he had seen the aircraft come down, had recognised it as the 'ndege' from Nyamaketi and been sure that it was searching for him.

He could see the pilot peering down from her cockpit and wondered whether this aircraft was part of the security force operation that had dogged his heels ever since he had entered the park. For three days, their pursuit had kept him moving and curtailed his hunting activities to such an extent that he carried the remains of only one bushbuck on his shoulder. Even that hapless beast had been a very thin bushbuck and hardly sufficient to feed a hungry family.

The poacher sighed unhappily. He too was desperately hungry. He hadn't eaten in days and his stomach griped painfully at the thought of sustenance. He knew the Makorokoro well and had hunted successfully around the pan on many previous occasions, but it seemed that even small antelope had been frightened off by the soldiers. Truly, life was becoming ever more difficult.

The poacher spat disdainfully in the dust as he thought about the men who were hunting him. They carried heavy rifles and wore fine uniforms of camouflage, but they were not men of the bush and he experienced little difficulty in staying ahead of them. Yet they would kill him if they could and leave his bones out for the hyenas to feast upon.

Now, after three days and one very thin bushbuck, he was heading back to his home across the river. In one hand, he carried the light spear with which he had killed the animal and on his back, the bushbuck itself – neatly butchered and wrapped in its own wet skin for easy

29

portage.

The skin would be cured and tanned by his womenfolk, while the flesh would be eked out to feed them all for another week. Then he would have to return on another hunting foray and the prospect made him curiously uneasy. He was a vastly experienced hunter, but the soldiers were many and in spite of their ineptitude, it was not entirely impossible that they would stumble upon him by accident. If that happened, he would die as other hunters and honey-gatherers had died, just for being in the national park. The anti poaching patrols knew no mercy and would shoot him out of hand.

The great park of Nata Pan was the only place where he could find food for his family and now it seemed that even the park was a hostile environment. Life, which had always seemed so simple, was becoming ever more difficult and dangerous.

The aeroplane dived silently down on his reverie and the poacher hurled himself into the thicket, ignoring thorns and sharp branches that tore at his skin. Crouching fearfully, he watched with his heart thumping at the narrowness of his escape.

It was only when the aeroplane was about to hit the water that the poacher realised that all was not as it ought to have been. The Piper was landing without wheels or propeller and he sucked in his breath. Surely, not even the finest of 'ndege' could come down on water?

Burying his face in wet mud as the aircraft hit the pan, the poacher shuddered with each successive, bouncing impact. Through a billowing curtain of spray, he heard sounds of rending metal and instinctively braced himself to run out and rescue the driver. If the man had survived, he must surely be badly hurt. He was on his feet and moving forward when common sense prevailed and he paused among the trees.

How would he explain his presence in this remote corner of the park – particularly at nightfall and with illegal meat and a bushbuck hide in his possession? Even if it had been a very thin bushbuck, the penalties for killing animals in the park were severe. He could not afford a fine and if he were locked up by the authorities, his family would starve.

With an almost imperceptible shrug, the poacher crawled back into his hiding place and watched to see what would happen.

Frowning deeply, he saw the pilot climb laboriously from the shadows and even through the gathering gloom, he could see blood soaking the bottom half of her overalls. Over the normal sounds attendant upon nightfall in the forest, he was aware of her whimpering cries and momentarily shook his head in disbelief. The driver of the 'ndege' was a woman. Surely this could not be. Even as he considered it, he wondered how he might turn Tracey's gender to his own advantage. Perhaps she might not be as unforgiving as her male colleagues. She was obviously badly hurt and women were surely slower to condemn than men.

Perhaps she might even forgive him for the very thin bushbuck. Better than that, she might have food of her own in the wrecked 'ndege'. His stomach growled tantalisingly at the thought.

From his hiding place, the poacher watched Tracey Kemp collapse in the mud and his face tightened in sympathy with her pain. Ingrained good nature urged him to help, but the voice of experience still whispered caution in the back of his mind. He would approach the girl only when the time was right and the hunting instincts, garnered in fifty or more poaching expeditions told him that this was not the moment.

Hitching the meat parcel further up his back, the

poacher continued his silent vigil. Long years of illegal hunting had endowed him with infinite patience and he knew, he had plenty of time.

***

Heavy rain drummed a monotonous tattoo on the metal roof of the building and churned the area around the offices into a sea of glutinous mud. Thunder rumbled violently and the wind blew stinging raindrops almost horizontally through the darkness. Jason Willard stood on the veranda with his research officer and cursed the weather. In the office behind them, the rangers sat in gloomy silence, the smoke of their cigarettes drifting in blue swirls around the light.

Restlessly, the big warden paced the wooden floor while Lewis watched in silent sympathy. The ecologist was desperately worried for Tracey Kemp, but for Willard, the position was infinitely worse. Under his grim facade, the warden had to be frantically upset and although Lewis did not always get on with his irascible boss, he could understand the senior man's pain.

"I should have been here, Man." The warden growled at Lewis. "I could have helped get her down. She should not have had to land alone and frightened, while I was absorbed in my own bloody useless problems."

Lewis merely nodded his head. There was nothing to say. Willard could indeed have been a comfort to Tracey when she needed it, but she was down now and there was no going back. Besides, he probably would not have had any more luck than Lewis himself when it came to getting through to the pilot on the VHF.

Jason Willard had spent the evening, watching elephants. A recent memo from Head Office had warned him that five hundred of the great beasts were to be culled that year and he had driven out to check on a herd that had

32

recently entered the park from across the river.

Like most men of the bush, Willard hated culling, but accepted that it was a necessary evil if elephant were to survive as a species. With less and less land available for the herds to wander, food would otherwise disappear and vast numbers of jumbo would starve to death. Other species would also suffer and culling was the only alternative. Feeling that as relative strangers, the new herd might cause him less heartache when the operation began, the warden had gone out to count them, only to find himself lost once more in the magic of being with wild elephants.

For Jason Willard, elephants were a true passion and he loved them with a fervour that bordered on the fanatical. Watching the great beasts in their natural state was a way to soothe his most troubled moments. They relaxed him with their supreme dignity, their acceptance of life's little problems and their unhurried love for one another.

They made him understand that his own troubles were very minor in the context of the wider world and by their dignified example, they gave him strength to face up to his personal difficulties. By walking among the beasts, he would probably have to kill, Jason Willard found it easier to live with his own feelings of guilt at being the agent of their destruction.

The moon had been high in the sky when rain drove him from the new herd and he wandered back to the Land Rover, soaked to the skin and weary, but once again confident in his own ability to cope. Returning to camp, he had discovered that in his absence, the person most dear to him had crashed in the dark Makorokoro and was probably lying injured and terrified while he was safe and sound in the comparative luxury of park headquarters. Although he knew it was probably illogical, Jason Willard did not like himself very much as he waited for the rain to stop.

***

Forty five kilometres from where the warden paced the floor, seven young men sat around a long wooden table. Above them, rain drummed on a tarpaulin sheet, water cascading down the supporting poles and puddles spreading visibly across the packed earth around the table. Supper was over and they glumly discussed the possibility of capturing another rhinoceros the following day.

"We won't get anywhere in this bloody weather," one bronzed young man offered moodily and others nodded in agreement. "Even if Jack can find the brutes in the thick stuff, we'll never get the trucks in to them."

He slapped irritably at a marauding mosquito and in a log palisade to one side of their makeshift dining room, a heavy horn smashed viciously into wood as one recent capture expressed his displeasure at being penned in. At almost the same moment, the men around the table were joined by a thickset man, who in spite of the darkness was wearing a broad-brimmed Stetson hat. Wiping moisture from his beard, he sat heavily down at one end of the table.

"That was the warden at Nyamaketi," he explained the radio call that had summoned him away from his dinner. "They've got a flying job for you at first light, Jack."

A millionaire industrialist from Minnesota, Randolph B. Claymore had set up and financed the rhino relocation exercise and although he was very much in charge, he was also part of the team. At his words, a painfully thin, red-headed man looked up from his coffee mug.

"Strewth Boss, what have you let me in for now? I'll never even get my Betsy off the ground in this stuff – not

34

without water wings at any rate."

Claymore smiled grimly.

"The park pilot has come down in the Makorokoro," he explained quietly and faces around the table suddenly tightened. "The warden thinks she would have made for the pan, but radio comms were bad and they cannot be sure."

"That is more than a little different, Boss."

Without more ado, Aussie Jack Meadows rose to his feet, in the process uncoiling a lanky frame of almost two metres. "I'll get a spare spotlight rigged and head for Nyamaketi as soon as possible."

"Hold it; hold it, Boy." The American growled. "A moment ago, you were burbling on about water wings, now you want to fly in the dark. I told the warden, you'd be there at first light, so relax."

The red-headed Australian shook his head.

Negative, Boss; if that pilot is down in the Makorokoro, he is in deep shit, so the sooner, I get mobile, the better. Strewth, Betsy and I can fly under water if there's a fellow aviator up a gum tree."

Without another word, the tall Australian hitched his cape around him and strode off into the darkness. A man of action himself, Claymore watched him go, a grim smile of approval flickering around his craggy features.

"That boy is mad," he observed to nobody in particular. "But if anyone can get airborne in this stuff, our Jack is the man. Let's just hope, he doesn't come to grief as well."

CHAPTER FOUR
(Aussie Jack)

The lion was in pain and the pain made him irritable and dangerous. The topaz eyes that glared out from the tangled thicket were misted with the agony of his ruined foot and to add to his problems, he was desperately hungry. With a two hundred and fifty kilogram frame to sustain, the great cat needed food and needed it badly.

Old and extremely experienced, the lion had lived on its own for nearly three years and had never experienced any difficulty in fending for itself. A poacher's snare had changed that. The cruel wire had clamped around the huge animals foot and for days, the lion had fought to free itself. One massive canine had snapped off in the struggle and the jungle killer had become ever weaker and ever more vulnerable to other predators.

Finally exerting all its remaining strength and ignoring the terrible agony of lacerating flesh, the lion had snapped the snare wire off at the base of the tree to which it was attached. One trailing end still followed the beast around, but at least it was free and could eat again.

But even that was difficult. The lion had lost the edge of its awesome speed and prey animals avoided its clumsy, hobbling rushes with ease. But the big cat did get the occasional meal. One baboon took foolhardiness to extremes by taunting the lion and paid with its life when a flailing forepaw crushed its skull like rotten papier-mâché.

But the meat on one baboon does little to assuage the hunger of a full grown lion and the ravenous jungle killer had set itself up in ambush on the edge of Makorokoro Pan, hoping that smaller animals could be waylaid on their way to water.

A major obstacle to this scheme was the fact that the

lion's injured foot had started to rot and the scent it gave off acted as a warning signal to lesser animals, so that they made wide detours to avoid the thicket in which the injured hunter lay.

The lion knew that if it did not feed soon, it would die and as it looked out on to the pan, hunger pains tore through its body. In waning daylight, it saw the aeroplane come down and the terrible cacophony of the crash drove it fleeing for its life, but like any cat, the lion had an insatiable curiosity. It was soon back among the trees on the edge of Makorokoro pan, from where it watched the injured pilot emerge from the wreckage of her aircraft. Instinctively, it noted her hobbling gait and smelled the blood, still oozing from her leg.

The scent brought saliva flooding into its mouth and the irony of the pilot's situation so closely mirroring its own was completely lost on the big animal.

Although the lion did not recognise Tracey Kemp as human, it sensed her pain and knew that she posed no threat to itself. With the infinite patience of its kind, the lion waited in silent anticipation for the meal that had so unexpectedly presented itself.

It knew that it would not be waiting long.

***

The poacher could see that the girl's condition was deteriorating fast. She lay with her face in the mud and had not moved for hours, although breath rasped noisily through her open mouth and little sobbing sounds issued from her throat.

Shifting uncertainly on his haunches, he wondered what to do. A feeling of imminent danger wafted like an elusive shadow across his scalp. Something was wrong, but he could not identify the cause of his unease. The rasping call of a hunting leopard echoed through the darkness, but he ignored the sound. The spotted killer was intent on other matters and for the moment at least, posed no danger.

There was something else and it was much closer than the leopard. The poacher was suddenly afraid and his fear was not for himself. The moon had disappeared behind heavy cloud and – his eyes aching with the strain – the poacher peered nervously into the night.

Almost without realising it, the poacher spotted the danger. Twenty metres to his right, a shadow moved. Even as he watched, it moved again – a smooth, almost imperceptible gliding motion that took it another metre closer to the prostrate pilot. As the lion gathered itself for the charge, the poacher leaped frantically to his feet. He had only seconds in which to act.

***

It was well after midnight and at last, the rain was easing when they heard the sound of an aircraft. Willard glanced up abruptly and Lewis turned towards him, their expressions identical in their bemusement.

There could be no mistaking the buzzing, 'whap, whap, whap' which was growing steadily louder. In spite of the storm, a helicopter was approaching. Willard yelled instructions as he sprang into action.

"Willie, get my Land Rover turned around and play the headlights on to the landing zone. Mark, you do the same with the cruiser. I don't know who this joker is, but if he can fly in this weather, he has to be the answer to our problems."

Even as whirling rotor blades slashed the rain-swept darkness above the office block, vehicle lights sprang into life and the warden heard the engine pitch change as a fragile aircraft wobbled from the stormy sky.

Seconds later, the chopper came solidly to rest and the turbine whine died away as the pilot cut the engine. A tall, angular figure jumped from the flimsy hull and ran across the mud, booted feet splashing and one hand holding down a wide-brimmed hat, sadly at risk from the wind.

Ignoring the weather, Willard and Lewis ran out to meet the newcomer. Aussie Jack Meadows greeted their astonished delight with a wide grin.

"Strewth Fellas, when the wet comes to these parts, it doesn't exactly dribble, does it? They call me Aussie Jack Meadows by the way and I gather you have an aircraft down somewhere nasty. After I've warmed my socks with a bucket of tea, I'm at your service."

His handshake was firm and his smile irrepressible as he regarded the parks men.

"That was an incredible bit of flying!" Lewis told him breathlessly and Willard nodded his agreement.

"It was thirsty work, Mate." The Australian modestly agreed and looked around pointedly while Lewis shouted for tea. Moments later, an orderly hurried in and while he poured, Willard studied the helicopter pilot.

Aussie Jack was a young man, very tall and cadaverously thin, but with a freckled face of such sublime innocence that he looked more like a candidate for choirboy honours than a hardened bush pilot. Vivid blue eyes returned the burly warden's frank appraisal and Aussie Jack smiled over his teacup.

"Tell me about it, Mr Willard. I reckon I have flown over most of your little kingdom and it is pretty shonky countryside to come down in, even without the wet."

Keeping his voice dispassionate, Jason Willard explained the situation. The Australian grinned tightly when he heard that the air force were unable to assist.

"Strewth, but that is typical of those buggers. They'll make any excuse not to fly at night. Their Alouettes are pretty ancient now and they don't have an artificial horizon fitted, so without daylight to help them, the Blue Jobs don't even know which way is up."

"And you?" Willard interjected. "I take it that your machine has the necessary instrumentation?"

Aussie Jack Meadows threw back his head and there was genuine amusement in his laugh.

"Strewth Warden, gimme a break willya. All I've got in my little egg-beater is fuel and temperature gauges. I wouldn't know how to use an artificial horizon if I had one I'm afraid. No, Man; I use the seat of my britches instead and it keeps me in one piece. At least, it has so far."

Willard shook his head somewhat doubtfully as he briefed the pilot further on Tracey's plight and the difficulties that would be faced in reaching Makorokoro pan by road. When he finished, the Australian fiddled absently with his hat, pulling the crown up into twin peaks and wrestling uneasily with the brim.

"Strewth, but I hate to sound sexist, Fellas," he said slowly, "but I reckon that your pilot being a sheila gives us even more of a problem. It would be bad enough if it was a bloke out there, but a girl….? Hell, I dunno."

He shook his head in obvious perplexity and his expression was suddenly bleak, but Jason Willard wasn't having that.

"Tracey is as good as any man when it comes to flying or survival in the bush." The warden began hotly, but Aussie Jack waved his objection aside. Sipping at his tea, the pilot went on in sober tones.

"Yeah, I'm sure she is, Warden, but still… Anyway, I can get my bird in there alright, provided I can find the crash site. The problem will be getting out with a load on board. Betsy is already as light as I can make her, but she wasn't built for passengers and in this weather, we could be in for a rough ride."

"It can't be much rougher than what you came in on," Lewis commented around his pipe. "You flew through a major storm to get here Jack, so surely, you can get in and out of Makorokoro once the rain subsides?"

The pilot looked pained.

"I can get in anywhere if I have to, Mr Lewis, rain or no rain. Coming here was easy because I knew the way, but I'll have to find Makorokoro pan and that will use up fuel by the bucket. My Betsy was designed to fly over farmland, not bloody great chunks of Africa. Even with full tanks when I leave here, we could be in trouble without refuelling somewhere along the line."

The three men pondered the problem, but it was Willie Sibanda who suggested a solution.

"Why not drop a drum off somewhere along the way, Boss? We could leave it in the middle of the main drag somewhere, so if Jack follows the road on his way out, he should be able to spot it."

"Good idea, Willie," the warden said shortly. "Right, I want you and Mark to take the Land Cruiser. Check out the mud flats at Tombekule and if there's nothing there, make for the pan.

'In the meantime, I'll go straight for Makorokoro with spare fuel for Jack's helicopter. We can rendezvous along the way once he has located the crash site and checked on Tracey's condition."

Jason Willard's face was suddenly tight with strain and his eyes looked haunted.

"Come on; come on: the rain has eased now, so let's get going. You too Jack: we are wasting precious time."

"Hold it a mo, Warden," the red-headed man stopped him with an imperiously raised hand. "I rushed across here in the wet because things sounded pretty damned desperate. As it turns out, I don't reckon another couple of hours will make too much difference and I'm not going to try for this Makorokoro place until I can see where I'm going. Strewth, my little Betsy may not be the grandest flying machine around, but she is all I own in the world."

"And Tracey is all I…."

Willard broke off his angry retort and looked helplessly at Jim Lewis.

"Jack is right, Jason," the ecologist agreed gently. He sympathised with the warden's impatience, but the pilot had a valid point. "It will be daylight in a few hours, so there isn't much point in taking the chopper up before then. The rain has almost stopped and we should be able to get both trucks moving pretty soon, but in the meantime, I'll lay on early breakfast, so that we can all start out on a decent footing."

In spite of his worries and the urgent need for haste, Willard knew that Lewis was right. The helicopter was the only hope for Tracey Kemp and to risk it unnecessarily was asking for trouble. Once the rain stopped, they could all get under way and thanks to the unorthodox Australian, help would surely be with Tracey within a few hours. The warden fervently hoped that nothing further could happen to her in that time.

Yet even as they all sat down to fried eggs and bacon, the injured pilot was facing yet another moment of very real danger.

CHAPTER FIVE
(Problems in the Mud)

Tracey Kemp was lost in a wonderland of dreams and hazy memory. Her mind, clouded by pain, she wandered through a gentle landscape, populated by wondrous animals and people from her past. Half formed memories drifted through her sub conscious and she smiled through her pain as they took her backward in time.

There he was – big Jason Willard, looking embarrassed and ill at ease in a smart suit when they attended a fancy function at the university. In contrast, she pictured him back in jungle greens and concentrating on the tracks of a particular leopard that he wanted her to see.

"See the way, he has started running, Tracey," the big man crouched on his haunches to point out how sand had been kicked up at the rear of each paw print when the animal broke into flight. Tracey had been fascinated, but more by the enthusiasm of her lover than by any arcane mysteries of tracking. Tracey's heart filled with remembered pride at the thought that this man – this renowned expert on wild animals – was hers and loved her as much as she loved him.

And there was the first occasion he had taken her out into the bush. They had camped on a knoll, not far from the capital city and Jason had spent an entire evening explaining the stars that lit up the night sky above them. He pointed out galaxies, clusters and individual comets, explaining their names, their histories and what they meant in legend and the tribal lore of so many African people.

On other occasions, he made her listen to the sounds of the night and taught her to interpret their meaning. There was a world of difference between the angry cough of a hunting lion and the sobbing grunt by which

'Shumba' tells the world that he is looking for love. With Jason, she heard the sawing rasp of leopard and learned to differentiate between the unearthly scream of hyrax and night ape, the yammering of jackal and the eerie giggle of foraging hyena. At first, the sounds were terrifying, but in time she had come to recognise exactly what they meant and love them as part of her own wild world.

"The lion is a vastly over rated beast," she could hear the big man's voice murmuring in her ear. She could see his ruggedly handsome face and felt a deep yearning to feel his arms around her – to feel the comfort he was so adept at imparting. In her dream, he turned towards her and she could see the glint of ironic humour in his eye.

"He is so big," Willard ignored her yearning and went on about the lion, "and so magnificently powerful that he has attracted the admiration of mankind throughout the ages. Yet, deep down inside, Shumba is just an overgrown tabby cat and like all his kind, he is fickle, idle and a terrible bully. He likes nothing better than to sleep in the sun with a full belly and in spite of his strength, he is seldom dangerous or aggressive towards man."

The deep, coughing grunt penetrated her consciousness and Tracey opened her eyes in wonderment. In the pale light of a waning moon, she could clearly see an immense, black-maned lion crouching not fifteen metres from where she lay. Even with its belly flattened to the ground, the beast looked enormous and Tracey's eyes opened even wider as it rose slowly to its feet. She couldn't help noticing with interest how the animal's massive chest tapered into rangy hindquarters to present an image of savage, natural grace. This was the epitome of a jungle killer, but Tracey felt no fear. Baleful, yellow eyes glared hotly into hers, but as the lion curled its upper lip in a silent snarl that exposed mighty canines, she had a sudden yearning to play with the fearsome creature, as once she might have played with a puppy.

Calling quietly to the killer cat, Tracey hesitantly held out one hand and the great, tufted tail lashed ominously from side to side. Dropping on to its belly once more, the lion flattened itself even closer to the wet earth. A tremor ran through its body as it braced itself for the charge, but Tracey Kemp did not notice or appreciate the danger. She longed to hold the great beast to her bosom and stroke its threadbare mane. She wished it would come closer and even thought about crawling across to meet it, but a deep lethargy enveloped her body and in any case, movement would only bring back the pain.

Wearily, she looked around for Jason Willard. Surely he would help. He should be there for her when she needed him so badly. It was his duty. But Willard was not there and her irritation mounted at his absence. Why was he never around when she needed him most? With a sigh of troubled frustration, Tracey Kemp forgot about the lion and dropped her head back on to the mud.

From the darkness of the forest, the poacher watched in mounting horror. He had been on the point of running at the lion when the girl raised her head and he felt a surge of relief that she had spotted the danger that threatened. In spite of his own anxiety, he wondered what she would do. As a game ranger – even one who drove the 'ndege' – she would surely be able to protect herself. Yet the lion was inching ever closer to her prostrate body and if she did not react very soon, she would just as surely die.

The poacher trembled with anxiety as he watched the drama unfold. It soon became apparent that the injured girl cared not one whit for the menacing cat. If she was afraid, she gave no sign of it and he felt an almost reverential awe for such raw courage. This was no ordinary woman, this driver of the 'ndege'. This was a woman who could face down a lion at close quarters without displaying the slightest hint of fear.

This was a woman who was going to get herself killed!

Suddenly realising that the pilot had drifted back into unconsciousness, the poacher rose silently to his feet. He had to do something. If he remained motionless in the darkness, he would be forced to witness the killing of this incredible woman and he could not allow that to happen. Emerging silently from his hiding place, he ran toward the menacing cat. In one hand, he carried his light spear poised for the throw and in his heart, he was sorely afraid. The puny blade was hardly suitable for facing down a lion, but it was all he had with which to defend himself and the woman.

Running silently over wet mud, the poacher saw great yellow eyes flicker at his approach and knew a momentary sense of triumph. For all its awesome size, the lion was even more afraid than he was himself.

"Hau Shumba," pausing only metres away from the giant beast, the poacher shouted his challenge. "You are a great hunter, but you cannot kill this incredibly brave woman. You must kill me first and I will not allow it."

The lion was an enormous specimen, but it was obviously in poor condition. In the moonlight, the poacher could see raw scars and festering scabs about its body where vicious thorn branches had torn at the pale hide. Wire dangled from one thick leg and he smelled the putrefaction that was spreading through the gigantic body. The beast was approaching the end of its life. Few creatures grow old in the African bush and for this particular hunting cat, time was running out. For all that, it was still terribly dangerous.

With less than five metres between them, man and beast faced each other in the fitful moonlight. Both of them were sorely afraid. Tawny eyes locked with fearful brown ones, but the lion's arrogant confidence had been weakened by hunger and pain. The unknown threat, posed by this shadowy figure from the night proved too much for the giant cat.

With a rumbling growl and a last, lashing flick from its tail, the lion spun around and disappeared into the trees in a series of awkwardly leaping bounds. Trembling violently with reaction to the closeness of his escape, the poacher looked down at the sleeping girl.

"Aieesh;" he thought to himself; "she is so beautiful and so young to be flying an 'ndege' herself. How can any such child have the courage to laugh at Shumba then go back to her sleep? Truly this woman is the bravest of the brave."

Shaking his head in baffled admiration, the poacher wondered whether perhaps the pilot had been killed when the aircraft crashed and this was but her Spirit, sleeping beside the water. Although she did not look like a Spirit, that would explain a great deal. But no, it could not be – Spirits felt no pain and the poacher had witnessed Tracey's agony with his own eyes. This was no Spirit. This was a flesh and blood woman who drove an 'ndege' and was badly hurt.

Shaking his head again, the poacher was about to return to his shelter among the trees when Tracey Kemp opened her eyes and saw him.

***

"Will you bloody well look at that lot!"

The muttered exclamation came from Mark Nicholson, sitting beside Sibanda in the Land Cruiser. Behind them, the game scouts peered over their shoulders, but the scene ahead was a depressing one. The road had disappeared and in its place was a surly torrent of brown water. The Avamure River – usually no more than a

47

muddy trickle – had burst its banks and heaving floodwater stretched ahead through the darkness like an enormous, rolling sea. In the headlights, they could see branches and even small trees floating swiftly downstream and Sibanda pounded the steering wheel in angry frustration.

"We must get across," he muttered. "If Tracey is down on the mud flats, she is going to be hurt and we have to reach her as soon as possible.

'What do you think, Mark?"

The younger ranger shook his head.

"We'll never make it, Willie. That water will be over a metre deep in places and look how fast it is flowing."

To prove his point, Nicholson climbed down from the truck and removed his boots before wading gingerly into the torrent. The others watched in silence and when the ranger was half way across, Willie Sibanda sprang into action.

"We can't just sit here, Fellas," he muttered to the scouts. "If Mark can walk it, then we can bloody well get through as well."

Roughly putting the big vehicle into gear, he followed his colleague into the water. Keeping the engine revs high with his foot, he concentrated on the wading figure ahead, his confidence rising by the moment. The water level stayed below Mark Nicholson's waist and that was nothing for the Land Cruiser. The tense silence behind him told that his passengers were not so sure.

As foam-flecked water rose against the wheels, so the vehicle began to shake to the steady battering of the swollen river. Boulders ground together in the flood and Sibanda concentrated on keeping the wheels in as straight a line as possible. Sweat trickled down his face and he felt every bump, stone and crevice beneath the tyres. When the Land Cruiser lurched, he prayed silently that the wheels would maintain their grip on the sodden riverbed. If they slipped sideways, neither he nor the scouts would stand a chance. The vehicle would be hurled downstream and they would all be dashed into oblivion by the force of the raging water.

"I just hope Tracey appreciates all this." Sibanda murmured aloud, but nobody heard him. Three pairs of eyes were staring intently at the surging waves, so graphically illustrated in the wavering headlights. An impala floated past, horns tangled in a mat of vegetation and its eyes shining blue in the headlight beam. Whether it was alive or dead, none of them could have said. Metre by tortured metre, the Land Cruiser lumbered through the flood. At one point, water flowed through the cab and both scouts raised their feet to avoid it. Floating debris crashed loudly against the doors and Sibanda prayed that no large trees would be washed down while they were crossing. His eyes ached with the strain of concentration and his hands were clamped on the steering wheel in a vice-like grip.

They had less than ten metres to go when disaster struck.

Mark Nicholson was already out of the water and turning towards them when the nearside, front wheel dropped into a hole. Almost in slow motion, the vehicle lurched to one side and as panic surged in his chest, Sibanda allowed his foot to slip from the accelerator.

While the engine was running hard, exhaust gases poured through the outlet pipe, keeping water out and allowing the Land Cruiser to keep going. As soon as the accelerator pressure eased, the gases diminished and were immediately overcome by the flood. Muddy brown water surged up the exhaust pipe and flooded the engine. The Land Cruiser coughed, backfired and spluttered to a stop.

For one long moment, the silence was absolute then Willie Sibanda groaned aloud as he frantically turned the ignition key again and again without getting the slightest sign of life from the drenched engine.

Almost on the point of tears, park ranger Willie Sibanda turned to his colleagues.

"Okay – out you two. We'll have to push her on to the bank and try to dry her off."

It took nearly forty minutes to manhandle the heavy vehicle clear of the floodwater and Nicholson immediately opened the bonnet, while his colleague turned sadly to the radio.

They were forty minutes that had been totally wasted and even more time would inevitably elapse before they could resume the search for Tracey Kemp.

***

Regional warden Philemon Makwata wore a worried frown as he climbed stiffly down from his vehicle. Jim Lewis hurried out to meet him and the two men shook hands.

Makwata had driven through the night in order to reach Nyamaketi as darkness faded into grey daylight. He was tired and sore, but Lewis gave him more bad news as they walked toward the offices.

"Willie Sibanda has come to grief near Tombekule, Sir," the ecologist said quietly. "It seems, he tried to cross a flooded drift on the Avamure and bogged down. I'm afraid it is going to take them a good hour or so to get going again.

'Not quite what we need at this stage, I'm afraid."

`The regional warden grunted moodily.

"You always were a master of understatement, Mr

Lewis. I suppose we do still have the warden's vehicle, do we?"

Lewis explained that Willard had left for the Makorokoro two hours before first light.

"He took the Land Rover with spare fuel for the chopper, Sir. If all goes well, he should reach the pan by late morning."

And the helicopter?"

"Refuelling down at the strip and due to take off about now."

Even as Lewis spoke, they heard the high-pitched clatter of the helicopter and moments later, the fragile little machine appeared above the trees. As the perspex bubble swooped overhead, they saw the pilot raise one hand in salute.

Philemon Makwata shook his head.

"You know, Mr Lewis," he said slowly, "I get the feeling that things are going badly wrong. Call me old fashioned if you like, but I have never believed that women should be allowed anywhere near expensive machinery.

'I was against Miss Kemp's appointment to the Air Wing from the start and it seems that events have proved me right."

"That is hardly fair, Sir," Lewis protested, but the regional warden silenced his objections with an upraised hand.

"Hear me out, Mr Lewis. Not only has our little lady in all probability written off an expensive aeroplane, but we now have a useless Land Cruiser and the warden has committed the department to an enormous amount of much needed money by using this helicopter, which is far too small for a rescue mission in any case.

'The Makorokoro is a place of Spirits, Man – we all

know that. Miss Kemp should have been left to take her chances until the air force arrives on the scene. They are the only people with the necessary equipment and expertise to get her out. All this going off half-cocked is just asking for trouble."

Sighing theatrically, the regional warden held his hands out, palm uppermost.

"What else can possibly go wrong, Mr Lewis?"

In spite of his worries, Jim Lewis couldn't help smiling. Makwata was merely letting off steam to relieve his own tension and the research officer recognised the tirade for what it was.

"Come inside and have a cup of tea, Mr Makwata." He suggested gently.

"Tea; tea – does this department run on ruddy tea?" The regional warden frowned heavily, although a spark of amusement flickered in his eyes. "Whenever anything goes wrong, Mr Lewis – we produce tea. If we want to celebrate – we have more tea. It is a wonder that the entire department isn't staffed by used tea bags.

'Mind you, I sometimes think that might be an improvement."

Laughing softly, Lewis followed the irascible senior officer into the office where in spite of his protestations, Regional Warden Philemon Makwata enjoyed an excellent cup of tea.

***

Tracey saw the man through a pain-filled haze. She had been dimly aware of his confrontation with the lion, but it all seemed part of a dream.

"Jason," she murmured sleepily, "I knew you wouldn't leave me here. Something went wrong with…."

Opening her eyes a little wider, she giggled with somewhat hysterical embarrassment.

"You're not, Jason. I'm sorry, but…."

Her voice tailed off and she struggled to stay awake.

To her sleepy mind, the poacher appeared a handsome man, a man of infinite bravery. He had proved his courage by chasing the lion away, even though the animal had meant her no harm. She was not sure why the cat had been there, but felt sure that it must have had something to do with her aeroplane.

Drifting off to sleep again, Tracey remembered the wonderful stories, her father had told her when she was little and smiled dreamily to herself. The bedtime story had always been a ritual in the Kemp household and she could remember Pops – she had always called him that – sitting on the end of her bed, sometimes reading from a book and sometimes making up the tales as he went along.

He had told her stories of Africa – of great animals and the men who hunted them. He had told her of personalities, both good and bad from the pages of her country's history. Mzilikazi, Lobengula and Selous – Ambuya Nehanda, Marondera and Allan Wilson, all were names that she readily remembered. Pops had also told her the legends and folk tales of Africa, interspersed with the fables of other lands and different cultures. She had thrilled to the exploits of those brave and handsome warriors of the Amaveni – Lobengula's personal bodyguard, who were individually selected for their good looks, their physique and their boundless courage. She had laughed with Rat, Mole and Brer Rabbit, then shuddered with distaste when Bere the hyena was wreaking havoc among the other animals.

A sensible girl, Tracey had been well aware that most such stories were vastly exaggerated. History has a knack of warping facts to suit the individual and she had laughed with her father when his tales were particularly far-fetched, yet it seemed that there might be a basis of fact in even the most unlikely fables. King Lobengula – the Great Black Bull of Matabele history – was long since dead and his grave had never been found. Yet here in the dark Makorokoro was one of his warriors running to her rescue with assegai in hand and ready to do battle.

Oh, he was so beautiful and she was such a lucky girl.

Giggling gently to herself, Tracey looked adoringly up at the stranger. He returned her gaze and made no move to speak and before she could say anything or express her thanks for his gallantry, oblivion overtook her once more and Tracey Kemp drifted back into sleep.

Watching her eyes close and realising that Nature was keeping her from as much pain as was possible, the poacher crouched beside the injured pilot, water splashing about his feet. He knew that she was terribly vulnerable where she lay and he had to get her into some form of shelter before the lion returned. Moving her without causing further pain was not going to be easy, but it had to be done. Carefully placing his arms under her legs and shoulders, he lifted Tracey carefully from her muddy bed. Her eyes opened briefly and she tried to smile, but one trailing foot caught on a broken branch and he saw agony flare in her eyes before she screamed aloud and blacked out again.

Murmuring unheard words of comfort to his distressed burden, the poacher carried her toward the trees. She was a dead weight and he was not a big man, but years of bush life had given him a strength that was not readily apparent in his skinny frame. Nevertheless, he staggered awkwardly beneath his load, although at last he was able to lay her down beneath a big mahogany tree that stood alone, twenty metres from the forest line. Carefully adjusting her position so that she lay on her back with the injured limb outstretched, he stood back and studied the injured pilot, wondering what else he could do.

The unconscious girl's face was drenched in sweat, while her hair was matted and wet. Even in the gloom, he noticed the bright spots of colour on her cheeks and felt a sense of deep foreboding at what they entailed. As he put his hand out to test her forehead for the fever that he knew was beginning to rampage through her system, the girl tossed her head from side to side, whimpering in her pain and digging her teeth deep into her lower lip, so that blood trickled down her chin.

Withdrawing his tentative hand, the poacher placed the bushbuck carcass carefully beneath her head as a makeshift pillow and shuffled his feet in indecision.

The girl was as comfortable as he could make her, but she needed proper medical help and that would not be available before daylight, even if the park authorities knew where she was. By then, it would almost certainly be far too late. The poacher had witnessed death in the bush on far too many occasions to have any doubt about that.

Without immediate help, the pilot would die.

Moving back into the shelter of the trees, the poacher squatted down on his haunches and watched the girl in her torment.

***

Although the rain had finally stopped, the sky was still dark and lowering as Jason Willard urged his vehicle toward the Makorokoro. He had already passed through a number of squally showers – each one, a solid curtain of water, slashed by ragged streaks of lightning – and knew that there were many more to come.

An expert in driving when conditions were bad, the

warden steered the heavily laden Land Rover with gentle hands, avoiding those darker patches on the road where water lurked beneath the mud. If he hit one of those, the best he could hope for was a bad skid – the worst, a wheel sinking up to the axle.

Preoccupied and deeply concerned for Tracey's safety, Willard drove by instinct and the game scout beside him made no effort to disturb his brooding concentration. The warden's thoughts were on Tracey Kemp and even as he drove the vehicle to its limits, he wondered how he could reach her even faster.

How he would have loved to accompany Aussie Jack Meadows in the helicopter, but that had obviously been impractical. Willard was a big man and even without the problems of fuel, the chopper was already stripped to its basics and had an almost impossibly tiny amount of passenger space. If Tracey was badly hurt as seemed likely, she would need a rapid air lift and that meant utilising all the space that was available.

Willard groaned inwardly as he pondered on the probability of Tracey being injured. He had once brought a light aircraft down on water and had escaped with severe bruising, but that had been in broad daylight and he had been incredibly lucky. To do the same thing in darkness and get away without serious injury would require an enormous amount of luck as well as supreme flying ability. Tracey must have been injured in the landing and Willard could only hope and pray that the Australian would be able to handle whatever first aid might be necessary.

Aussie Jack had laughed aloud when the warden questioned his abilities in this regard.

"Strewth Warden, I was a jackaroo before I started flying aeroplanes. I've been patching up busted drovers and fighting drunks since I was barely out of nappies. I will cope with your little lady, whatever the problem."

Willard had not the slightest idea what a jackaroo might be and remained unconvinced. In spite of his obvious competence in the air, the red-headed Australian seemed absurdly young and his look of cherubic innocence did little to inspire confidence in the harsh world of the Nata Valley.

But for all Jason Willard's doubts, Aussie Jack was in his element. Flying twenty metres above the Mopani scrub, he followed the winding red strip of mud that was the main road to Makorokoro and whistled cheerfully to himself. Kicking the helicopter on to its side, he detoured on occasion to watch vast herds of elephant and at one point, an old buffalo bull standing motionless beside a rhinoceros in a mud wallow.

"Strewth, but that is a fair bonzer sight," he muttered aloud to himself. "I reckon, those two must be buddies from way back or somethin'."

Resuming his original line of flight, the Australian flew on toward Makorokoro, still whistling under his breath and cheerful in spite of the circumstances. Spotting Jason Willard's Land Rover struggling through the mud below, he swooped down on the vehicle to give the warden a little encouragement. One beefy arm appeared through the window in a brief wave, before Willard's attention was returned to the road conditions.

Although he had no inkling of what lay ahead, Aussie Jack Meadows was flying straight into trouble.

CHAPTER SIX
(Down in the Makorokoro)

The great bull moved ponderously through the trees. At seventy years of age, he was an immense figure of majestic dignity. Standing taller than the average city dwelling, he weighed in excess of six tonnes and the tusks that jutted from his jaw were enormous by any standards. They dropped away from his leathery face in creamy magnificence and were the reason for the broad, leather collar that snuggled unobtrusively around the elephant's neck.

In the collar, a tiny radio transmitter gave off a continuous signal, clearly read on instruments, carried in the park aircraft – that same, brokenly useless machine that lay in twenty centimetres of murky water at the edge of Makorokoro Pan.

The elephant knew nothing about collars or radio transmitters. He had grown accustomed to the aircraft and ignored its daily pestering, but as he moved through the fading night, a feeling of deep unease made him restless and dissatisfied.

Throughout his long life, the bull had lived in the Makorokoro, close to the river. The riverine vegetation provided him with shelter and food, while he enjoyed having plentiful water always close to hand. On occasion, he was joined by younger bulls, eager to learn about life as a solitary tusker. He taught them all he knew and when they were sufficiently prepared for survival in the bush, sent them on their way with heavy blows from his trunk and much harsh prodding from those mighty tusks.

For a few years, the elephant had lived with another bull, every bit as large as himself although the other beast carried no ivory. In time, the tuskless one had also moved on and the bull had been left alone to live out his life in quiet dignity. He spent his days, wandering the valley floor, generally unthreatened, but his instinct for danger was acute and this was what had ensured his survival through the years.

In truth, there was little to threaten any elephant in the National Park – with the possible exception of Man himself. The bull had been hunted by men on many occasions and recognised the threat. His tusks made him a natural target for every poacher, south of the great desert and he had been attacked with spears, arrows and automatic weapons. He had narrowly avoided pit traps and contemptuously torn apart the cruel wire snares that had settled around his legs.

He had survived every danger and in the survival, his reputation had grown and his tusks had assumed ever greater value. Those huge pillars of ivory acted as a natural magnet to the men with guns and this constant threat to his well being had developed in the bull, an uncanny sense of danger. Wandering restlessly among the wet Mopani trees, the great beast searched the atmosphere with a nervously questing trunk. There was trouble about in the dark bush and he felt deeply uneasy. On one side of his right tusk, a jagged piece of ivory had been torn away by a viciously tumbling bullet and in the depths of this strange wound, a miniscule portion of nerve was exposed to the air. Over the years since the injury had occurred, the tusk had rarely given him trouble, but when it did, the pain always seemed to coincide with his periods of unease. As he walked, the elephant threw his head fretfully about, sail-like ears cracking like pistol shots in the silent forest.

As he invariably did when danger threatened, the bull made his way into an area of tangled jess bush that prevented access to all but the most horny-hided of beasts. As he drew closer to the dark waters of Makorokoro Pan, the thorn scrub became ever denser around him and eventually, he halted beneath a giant tamarind tree that provided an ideal position of vantage for an ambush.

Here he would wait and when danger eventually showed itself – as he knew it would – the old bull would be ready for it.

***

If he had been asked, Aussie Jack Meadows would have cheerfully admitted to being anything but a brave man. He led an adventurous life and enjoyed pitting his skills against the elements, but true courage lies in the ability to conquer fear. Meadows was one of those rare beings, born without that particular emotion and so what passed for bravery was merely his way of bringing excitement to what might otherwise have been a fairly routine existence.

Born the youngest son of an Australian stockman, Jack had been brought up in the harsh, dry world of the Northern Territories. At an age when his peers were struggling with their mathematical tables, Jack had been mustering cattle and even among the tough drovers of the Outback stations, he had quickly built up a reputation for daring.

But Jack had never wanted to spend his life on a permanent cattle trail. That was for morons as far as he was concerned. Jack wanted to fly. Smitten with the aviation bug as a twelve year old, he had saved every penny he earned to put himself through flying school and then eked out a meagre living as an airborne cowboy, driving the same cattle from a helicopter rather than a horse or pickup truck.

It was hard, demanding work, but Jack enjoyed the life and in his leisure time, he built his own helicopter out of spare parts and a few pieces of ingeniously worked aluminium or plastic. Few people expected the ungainly machine to actually fly, but when Jack finally lifted it from the ground and flew around the station on which he was working, his colleagues gave a ragged cheer and opened more beer in celebration.

Owning his own machine, gave Jack the opportunity to branch out on his own and having set himself up as a freelance crop sprayer, he had soon been in demand throughout the Northern Territories. From Darwin to Van Diemen's Land, everyone wanted Aussie Jack Meadows and his quaint little aircraft, not only for the skill and daring he brought to the work, but also for his cheerful personality. There was also the fact that he readily admitted to being 'the best ruddy crop duster in the whole of Oz.'

But for Jack, life was a matter of challenge and the money, he earned was irrelevant. A near fatal crash while showing off to a stockman's pretty, blonde daughter eventually destroyed his home-made helicopter, but by then, he had enough money put by to invest in a brand new machine from France. The Gazelle had the additional advantage of being able to fly on ordinary aviation fuel, rather than the 'avtur' mixture, used by older helicopters.

With the challenges of his homeland beginning to wane, Aussie Jack – by then, a veteran of almost twenty three years - shipped his new machine to Africa in search of adventure in a different environment. The challenge of bush life appealed to the young Australian and he was soon in demand again, particularly in remote areas where wild animals were to be found, counted and sometimes culled or relocated. With the passage of time, Jack had mellowed slightly and although he still flew his aircraft under telegraph wires or landed in apparently inaccessible terrain because someone else said it was impossible, he took few genuine risks and had developed into a very fine bush pilot.

Aussie Jack Meadows didn't know Tracey Kemp, but

he had no hesitation in flying to her rescue. Like most aviators, he often thought about finding himself in a similar predicament and when he had learned that the downed pilot was female, his own ingrained chauvinism displayed itself in unstinted admiration.

"Strewth Warden, I don't reckon, I ever heard of a sheila flying bush before," he told Jason Willard over breakfast. "She must be one hell of a girl."

"She is;" Willard agreed moodily; "Tracey is a girl in a million."

The rain had died away by the time Jack took off, but heavy clouds to the east told of more storms to come. The Australian was flying directly toward the rough weather and his normally cheerful countenance was grimly serious as he steered his flying machine into the murk.

"Okay, Little Lady: here we go."

But whether he was talking to his aircraft or the downed pilot in Makorokoro, only Aussie Jack knew for certain.

It wasn't long after he 'buzzed' Willard's vehicle that he had trouble of his own to contend with. An ear-splitting explosion sounded from above his head and although he was not prone to emotion, Aussie Jack frowned as he squinted up into the workings of the spinning rotor.

"Hey up." He muttered to himself.

With his lower lip gripped tightly between his teeth, the Australian glanced anxiously across the instrument panel and considered his options. Although the control lever felt firm in his hands, there was obviously something very wrong and he automatically scanned the surrounding countryside in case he needed to land in a hurry.

Above his head, the motor gave an asthmatic cough and then another before the thunderous explosion was repeated. The rotor blade seemed to hesitate momentarily on its axis and the pilot's hands blurred as he checked switches, levers and pulleys in his efforts to identify the problem. The helicopter was less than ten metres above the treetops and dark Mopani forest spread like a vast, unbroken blanket over the earth below.

"You've got yourself in a pretty bind this time, Boy," Jack told himself unnecessarily. "I reckon, it has to be a problem with the fuel and if it doesn't clear itself in a hurry, you're gonna have to put her down somewhere."

Like many men who spend long periods alone, Jack liked to talk aloud to himself, not only for the illusion of company, but also because it helped to clear his mind in an emergency. Although the words were spoken with calm deliberation, his eyes were continually on the move while his hands made rapid adjustments to the controls.

Away to his left, Jack could see the river gleaming silver in fitful sunlight. The road was no longer in view, but that didn't worry him unduly. The helicopter was small and there were a number of clearings in the forest where he could land without too much difficulty, but he was annoyed that anything should go wrong at that stage.

"It has to be shonky fuel in those drums," he muttered to himself. "A hundred bucks to a rotten apricot, those dingoes at Nyamaketi never bother to check them out. That is probably why the lassie came down as well."

Fuel supplies in remote bush stations were often inclined to remain unused way past their 'sell by' date and were prone to contamination, often from the drums themselves. Meadows normally made a habit of personally checking the avgas, put into his tanks but in the excitement of the morning, he had left the job to an attendant. Now he bitterly regretted his inattention to basic detail.

But it was far too late for regrets. After four minutes

of splutteringly erratic progress, the Australian spotted a large clearing away to his right with what appeared to be a rhino palisade in one corner. Having worked for nearly three months on the relocation programme, Jack recognised the pen for what it was and somewhat sadly wondered how many rhino were actually left in the area. However, the clearing offered ample space for a landing and he banked the crippled helicopter towards it. Bushes and small trees bucked in the wash of the descending rotor and mud splashed wetly as the wheels thudded solidly on to the ground.

"Not a bad landing in the circumstances, Sport." The Australian told himself with grim satisfaction. "Now let's check out the problem, hey."

He had little time for repairs however. Leaping lightly from the doorless cockpit with a large spanner in one hand, he looked up to see an enormous elephant burst from the trees less than thirty metres away.

The beast was obviously upset and Jack hesitated momentarily before flattening himself against the flimsy frame of his aircraft. The elephant towered above him. Searching the air with a nervously waving trunk, it spread its ears wide from the sides of its head. Pig-like eyes squinted short-sightedly around the clearing and when the enormous animal spotted the puny frame of a man standing uncertainly beside his machine, it let out a squeal of demented fury.

After a momentary pause to assess the dangers involved, the elephant pinned its ears to the side of its head, curled its trunk beneath a bristly chin and charged.

In spite of his reputation as an intrepid aviator without an iota of fear in his body, Aussie Jack Meadows dropped his spanner, whipped the hat from his head and ran for his life.

CHAPTER SEVEN
(A New Day Begins)

The poacher was desperately worried. If he dallied much longer, the police patrol must surely catch up with him and then his freedom would be forfeit. The only reason for his avoidance of capture over the years was the fact that he kept on the move – an elusive shadow flitting among the trees, seldom seen and never heard. Now he was trapped in one place by the injured pilot and mounting nervousness vied with his concern for her welfare.

After he had made Tracey as comfortable as possible and she had drifted back into sleep, the poacher built a small fire and squatted beside it, not only for warmth, but to give the pilot a bit of reassurance should she wake up suddenly. Light rain soaked into his threadbare clothing, but he showed no sign of discomfort and merely stared stoically into the darkness, his mind on other matters.

Apart from the injured pilot, the most pressing of his problems was concern for his family. Successive years of drought had left them destitute and they relied upon his hunting prowess to keep them alive. Two wives, an elderly mother and nine children – including two belonging to his late brother – all looked to him for food and the responsibility weighed heavily on his narrow shoulders.

He could not allow himself to be captured or killed. The injured girl would have to look out for herself. His mind made up, the poacher kicked irritably at the embers of his fire and replaced one log that had burned right through. Still he could not bring himself to leave.

The night hours passed slowly and as the sky lightened in the East, he removed a strip of meat from the pilot's makeshift pillow. It was blackened on the outside, although dried blood showed pinkly within. Sleepy flies had gathered on the morsel and flew irritably away as he prepared it for cooking.

The meat was for his family and their need was desperate, but he could not abandon this woman to her fate without doing something to make her more comfortable. Food was all he had to give, but his heart was sore as he contemplated the offering. It wasn't much, but it would feed one of his children for three days. His own stomach was tight with hunger, but that was of minor concern. He could go for days without sustenance, but the girl was moaning again, her condition obviously deteriorating. The meat could only do her good.

Shrugging with weary resignation, the poacher moved back to the fire. He could always kill another bushbuck.

The rain which had bedevilled the early hours had ceased, although heavy clouds lowered over the pan, their dark undersides streaked with surly lightning. Behind him, the girl cried out in her sleep as the Makorokoro prepared for the day ahead. A band of orange showed above the Eastern horizon and a lone hyena howled a noisy farewell to the darkness. Guinea fowl chinkled sleepily and jackals squabbled like fretful puppies over the remains of a kill. Almost imperceptibly, daylight drifted across the landscape.

Without bothering to clean the meat, the poacher impaled the morsel on a long stick and propped this makeshift toasting fork over the fire. Blood hissed and spluttered as it dripped into the coals and the aroma of roasting flesh brought saliva to the hungry man's mouth. His stomach griped angrily and for a moment, he thought he would pass out from the torment.

The smell added to his uneasiness. The morning air was very still and there was no breeze to carry a scent, but the pungent whiff of roasting meat would permeate through the bush and act as a beacon for patrolling representatives of law and order. Man is the only animal who cooks his food and the only men likely to be in this remote area of the park were there illegally. The poacher understood this and prayed to the Spirits of his people that the girl would soon wake, so that he could feed her and move on.

Once, he had made her comfortable, the poacher would be on his way. He was less than five kilometres from the river, where his home made canoe was hidden amongst the reeds. Had it not been for the 'ndege' coming down the previous evening, he would have been there already. He could yet be safe by the time the sun was at its zenith and he yearned to be moving. Makorokoro Pan had an evil history and the restless spirits of dead men did little for his rapidly waning sense of security.

The meat sizzled and burned above the fire; the rising sun grew closer to the moment when it would burst through the horizon and those creatures that made the Makorokoro their home stirred and shuffled as they prepared for the new day.

Behind the anxious poacher, Tracey Kemp moaned through painful dreams.

***

'Gerrupwillyer!'

The francolins cackling cry cut through Tracey's stupefied mind and she struggled to bring herself back to reality. Other francolin took up the morning call and giant, ground hornbills spoke to each other, their booming calls like the tympani of distant drums.

For long moments, Tracey did not have the slightest idea where she was. As memory began to return, she shook her head from side to side in her distress. She remembered trouble with the aircraft and the shuddering upheaval of coming down on the pan, but she could remember nothing after that. Somehow she must have dragged herself away from the aeroplane and the water, but the details were lost in a haze of pain. Groaning with the effort, she fought to dredge up blurred scraps from her memory.

A lion: there had been a lion. Frowning in deep concentration, she bit down on her lip as little by little, recollection returned. She pictured the great beast, a wispy mane darkening its shoulder and fearsome canines gleaming in the moonlight. She remembered the man – her unknown hero charging so bravely to her rescue. He had been so handsome, so strong and so brave…. Surely it had all been a dream.

Shaking her head in weary acknowledgement of her own foolishness, Tracey opened her eyes to discover that at least some of her dream had been based on fact. There had indeed been a man and he squatted on his heels beside a small fire while the smell of roasting meat brought saliva flooding into her mouth.

Struggling to sit up, Tracey gasped at the pain coursing through her body. Although she bit off the cry that rose in her throat, the stifled sound brought the man hurriedly to his feet. He glanced anxiously across at her and the tension in his thin body told her that he was on the point of flight. Weekly, she held up one hand to stop him.

Who the man was, she had no way of knowing, but he was hardly the Adonis of her dreams. In the shallow daylight, he was anything but handsome and definitely no great warrior of the Amaveni or any other fighting regiment. His face was lined and wrinkled, although he could not have been more than thirty five years old. His clothing hung in threadbare wisps from an extraordinarily small frame and even from four metres away, Tracey was aware of a rank, gamy smell emanating from his body. It caught in her throat, making her want to gag.

The little man spoke softly, but she could not understand the language he used. Shaking her head, she tried speaking to him in Chishona, of which she had a rudimentary knowledge, but he looked equally confused.

"Hello;" she searched for the words and gestured toward the fire. "Are you making breakfast?"

He obviously did not understand, so she tried again in English and the few words, she knew of the dialect, used by the valley inhabitants. None of them had any effect and subsiding into silence, Tracey smiled at the man and gestured at her lips with one hand. This time, his eyes lit up and his mouth opened in a gap-toothed grin.

"Nyama." He muttered briefly and that she could understand. 'Nyama' is the word for meat in just about every indigenous language, south of Khartoum and is instantly recognisable to any resident of Africa.

Smiling again, she nodded enthusiastically and patted her stomach. The man was ugly and he smelled bad, but he obviously meant her no harm and any human company was welcome in her predicament. Besides, the aroma of roasting meat was unbelievably pleasant in the morning air and although she was not hungry, Tracey savoured the prospect of a hot breakfast.

Even as she thought about it, the sun burst like a giant red fireball through the eastern rim of the world. As its rays sliced through the filmy wisps of night mist that still lingered above the water, the great, golden orb coloured them with its own crimson hue. For one brief moment, the dark and notorious Makorokoro – crocodile infested and with a history of violent death – looked as soft and innocent as a little girl's bedroom. In spite of her pain, Tracey held her breath in silent wonder, but the moment of beauty lasted only a few seconds. As the sun rose, its searing heat dissolved the soft pink vapour, whipping it from the water surface as though it had never been.

Momentarily forgetting her more pressing worries, Tracey shook her head in disappointment at the loss of something infinitely precious – if only for its rarity.

Bringing herself reluctantly back to the present, she saw the stranger crouching on his haunches two metres away. Hesitantly, he held a chunk of steaming red meat towards her. Smiling a little uncertainly, he urged her to take it with little jerking movements of his hand. Gesturing her thanks, Tracey reached out awkwardly, but the meat was blisteringly hot and she jerked her hand away with a cry of pain. The meat fell on to the ground and raw agony exploded in her leg at the sudden movement. The poacher rescued the meat with a vaguely reproachful look on his face, but his heart was sore at his own clumsiness and his eyes reflected deep concern at the stricken girl's obvious pain.

Stifling a groan and cradling her injured limb with both hands, Tracey shifted herself slowly into a more comfortable position while the man watched in impassive silence, the meat dripping hot blood over his hands. Feeling suddenly ravenous, Tracey reached out again and took the morsel from his outstretched fingers. Carefully dividing the hot meat into two equal pieces, she handed one to the man, but he shook his head and pushed it back towards her.

"No, you must have it," Tracey insisted, surprised to hear the weakness in her own voice. "It is for both of us."

Whether he accepted the firmness of her resolve or was just too hungry to argue, the man suddenly snatched the offered morsel and stuffed it into his mouth. He ate without finesse and blood ran down his chin, but his eyes dimmed with the delights of sustenance. Tracey smiled uncertainly before nibbling at her own portion. The man was obviously starving and she felt an increasing sense of guilt at taking what was theoretically his, even though his possession of fresh meat told her exactly what he was doing in this remote area of the park

The man was a poacher – that much was obvious. He was officially her enemy and in different circumstances, she would have been obliged to place him under arrest. Indeed, according to the law of the land, she would have been quite justified in shooting him. It was nearly eight years since the government had introduced draconian measures to combat the ever increasing poaching problem and many of those who hunted illegally had been gunned down without mercy. Others had received lengthy jail terms on appearing before the courts. This particular individual was one of those, designated a criminal and Tracey knew, she had no right to accept a share of his ill-gotten gains, no matter how hungry or hurt she happened to be.

She wondered what Jason Willard would make of the situation and the thought made her ache with longing for the big man's comforting presence. He had become so much a part of her life over the years and his pride in her achievements had spurred her on to ever more effort. Without him, she felt useless and inept. The warden was her friend, as well as the man who loved her and Tracey knew that he would be frantic with worry.

Tears sprang to her eyes at the thought that she might die and never see Jason Willard again. Worse still, if she died out here in the bush, she would leave him alone and unloved. His life had been very basic before she became part of it and she knew that he needed her to look after him. With a little grunt of determination, Tracey decided that she would survive, no matter what pain or suffering, she might be forced to endure. She would survive for Jason as well as herself and in surviving, she would make him realise just how much he needed her as a wife as well as a lover. No matter how much it hurt, she would be there for the warden when he needed her.

And pain there would certainly be – Tracey knew that only too well. Already, it was creeping through her leg again and threatening to devour her entire being. It was a nagging intensity of aching discomfort that seared into screaming agony with every untoward movement of her injured leg. In spite of her determination to survive, Tracey was suddenly unsure whether she could cope much longer and bitterly regretted waking up. While she had been asleep, she had at least been unaware of the agony.

Tearful and suddenly filled with self pity, Tracey chewed listlessly on her illegal breakfast. The meat was charred on the outside and raw within, but it tasted surprisingly good and although it was terribly tough, it would surely bring strength to her system. As she ate, Tracey couldn't help wondering what hapless animal had died to provide the meal.

The poacher watched her anxiously. His thoughts were as confused as those of Tracey Kemp. As far as he was concerned, he had done his duty toward the injured pilot and could move on with a clear conscience. With the onset of daylight, she would surely be safe and the longer he stayed with her, the more dangerous his own position became. To move on would show sound common sense, but still he was reluctant to leave the injured girl to fend for herself. After all, this was very wild countryside and she was only a woman.

African tribal society has always been rabidly misogynistic and women were looked on as lesser beings in every department. The thought that any female could possibly survive in the wild Makorokoro, even without the terrible injuries that this one had sustained did not occur to the poacher. And yet this driver of the 'ndege' had already demonstrated that she was more than just a woman.

Shaking his head in wry amusement at his own foolishness, the poacher glanced at the sable head insignia of the Parks Department, stitched on the left breast of Tracey's flying suit. She might be only a girl: she might be hurt and alone, but she was still a game ranger and therefore his enemy. Given the opportunity, she would arrest him and then what would become of his family? Without him to fend for them all, they surely could not survive.

His face wrinkled in thought, the poacher reflected anxiously on the alternatives that faced him. If he stayed, he must surely be caught – if not by the patrols already hunting him, then by those who would eventually arrive to rescue the pilot. They probably wouldn't shoot him, but would certainly lock him up and that would lead to the same result. He would not be able to survive in captivity and his family would still be left without a man and without protection.

On the other hand, if he left the pilot and resumed his journey home, could she possibly survive? It was true that she had already proved herself brave and resourceful, but she was very young and probably unversed in the ways of the bush. Had he not been present during the night, she would surely have been taken by the lion – that monster of the darkness, which had menaced them both and would have killed her without compunction. The cat had gone, but the Makorokoro was filled with other beasts, equally as large and every bit as dangerous.

Besides, the girl was still in great pain and her need for medical attention was becoming ever more urgent. The poacher knew of an excellent 'nganga' or traditional healer who lived across the river, barely twenty kilometres away, but he had no hope of transporting the girl even a fraction of that distance. Looking at her through downcast eyes as she ate, he noticed that her face was becoming blotchy with diffused blood and she was sweating considerably, He recognised the signs. Already, tiny 'skellums' of infection would be racing around her bloodstream and if she was not tended soon, she would almost certainly die.

There were also the armed patrols to consider. The men who had been pursuing him for the past three days. They were servants of the government and in some ways, colleagues of the injured pilot, but they were also soldiers and they were men. Men who lived in wild places and knew no law other than the law of conflict and the rules, they made themselves. Would this beautiful young woman be safe in the hands of such men?

The poacher shook his head in anxious bewilderment. He did not know what to do and so he hesitated, waiting for he knew not what.

Her impromptu breakfast completed, Tracey wiped dry lips on the sleeve of her overalls. It had hardly been five star cuisine, but it had been filling and she felt infinitely better for the sustenance. With food in her stomach, her pain seemed to have subsided into a dull, throbbing ache and for that she was grateful. She wanted to thank the poacher for sharing the meal with her, but without a common language, it was going to be difficult.

In fact, it was he who spoke first and although he used his own language, Tracey answered in English and for a moment, wondered whether he had in fact understood what she was saying. He was obviously curious about the aircraft in the water and she tried to explain what had happened. Speaking very slowly and using her hands to illustrate the words, she could see that he was struggling to comprehend. His eyes were crinkled in concentration and although she found it frustrating not to be sure that he understood, she completed the story of the wrecked Piper, then went on to question him about his family. Much to her surprise, he seemed to understand and with a bit of ingenuity, she was almost able to follow his reply. In this way – patiently and with many pauses to clear up a point – two people, totally foreign to each other, holding opposing ideologies and living vastly different lives – came to hold a stilted conversation.

In her efforts to communicate, Tracey forgot her pain and in his own sense of intrigue at speaking with this incredible young woman, the poacher lost his fear of imminent capture.

For Tracey, the laboured conversation merely added to the ambivalence of her feelings. The man was a poacher – a sworn enemy to any conscientious game ranger. He made no attempt to deny or disguise his illegal activities, even though he must have realised that she was a member of the Parks Department. At the same time, he was not one of the modern Kalashnikov carriers who slaughtered great beasts for their horn or tusks, leaving entire carcasses to rot where they lay. He was not one of those who threatened the very survival of the elephant and rhinoceros herds that were so integral a part of her world.

No – although this man hunted illegally in the park, he hunted only for food and his weapons were spear, bow and hunting knife. He used no cruel snares and she could understand his need to feed those who were his kin. In spite of the fact that he was killing beasts that ought to have been protected, Tracey recognised the fact that he had no alternative.

While the pain in her leg gradually built up again, Tracey tried to concentrate her mind on the dilemma faced by men such as this smelly poacher.

As a game ranger, she had always been totally dedicated to her job. Wild life held a deep fascination for her and Jason Willard's gentle teaching had made her into a dedicated conservationist. Like most members of the Parks Department, she found the concept of poaching a terrible one and recognised that criminals were steadily wiping out the animals that were the heritage of all mankind. This in itself was cause for grave concern, but for the first time, a tiny sliver of doubt stirred in Tracey's mind. The man beside her was no felon. He broke the law it was true, but he broke it honestly if that could be possible and did no lasting harm to wild life in the park. He surely did not deserve to be shot out of hand as so many poachers had already been shot.

It all seemed terribly confusing and Tracey struggled to reconcile the conflicting aspects of the problem.

Around them, the sun began to dry out the landscape, but neither the ranger nor the poacher was really aware of the change, even when the gathering heat began to make its effects felt on Tracey's gentle skin.

**

The elephant made no sound as it charged. Towering above the fleeing airman like a mobile skyscraper, it concentrated on the chase and wet mud flew from the impact of mighty feet.

Aussie Jack Meadows also ran in silence. His red hair shone brightly in the sunshine and his feet flew across the mud as he made for the dubious safety of the rhino stockade. As always, the adrenaline rush of danger excited him and he waved his hat in triumph as he launched himself over the heavy poles. Scrabbling away from the barrier, he slipped and fell full length in the sticky mud. Wiping muck from his eyes, he scrambled to his feet and turned to face the vengeful pachyderm, a scornful laugh on his lips.

"Come on then, ya great lumbering buffoon. See what

you can do about that then."

The elephant screamed an angry response.

The bull had been dozing when the descending helicopter backfired only metres above the forest. It had been the sound of a shot and enough to galvanise the massive beast into angry reaction. Screaming with rage, the bull charged powerfully through the trees, smaller branches shattering before its progress and thorny jess bush doing nothing to slow it down. Although the bull had no idea what it was chasing, it had an overpowering urge to destroy whatever it was that so noisily menaced its peaceful life.

Bursting into a large clearing, the mighty elephant had immediately seen the airman and after only a few moments of hesitation it, launched itself into a killing charge.

Having never been captured itself, the bull did not recognise the holding pen for what it was, but immediately sensed its strength. The stockade had been built with stout Mopani poles and was designed to withstand the onslaught of angry rhinoceros. Although it would not have kept a determined elephant at bay for long, it provided formidable protection for the fleeing airman. Slowing its charge at the very last moment, the bull skidded to a muddy halt and its mighty backside swung around to crash heavily against the barrier. The entire structure shuddered and Aussie Jack glanced quickly around to see where else he could run.

The second attack was a half hearted one and although the palisade shook violently, the collision with unyielding woodwork hurt the elephant without shifting the heavy poles. With a scream of baffled fury, the animal wheeled to move purposefully toward the centre of the clearing.

"G'arn then, ya great, lumbering bludger." Aussie Jack yelled feelingly after the determined beast. Wiping sticky red mud from his features, he jammed the bush hat back on to his head and opened his mouth to yell further abuse at the bull. This time, the words seemed to stick in his throat. An expression of horror flitted across his face as the elephant's intention became suddenly clear.

The bull was still angry and having been foiled in its efforts to vent that anger on the fleeing Australian, was bearing down on the only other creature that might provide satisfaction.

The immense bulk of the vengeful pachyderm moved with ponderous determination toward the flimsy frame of Jack's helicopter and there was a long moment of silence in the forest as it paused above it.

With a shout of indignant anger, the bush pilot sprang into precipitate action.

CHAPTER EIGHT
(A Curious Confrontation)

The sergeant was a veteran of war against the poachers. A patrol commander in the police Support Unit, he had worked in the Nata valley for many months and knew every square metre of the Makorokoro.

His patrol had been following a single poacher for nearly seventy two hours, before losing the man's tracks, late the previous afternoon. Two hours later, the sergeant had spotted the park aircraft flying low over Makorokoro Pan and his mood had instantly lightened. At the time, he and his men had been too far away to realise that the Piper was in trouble and his first thought was that the pilot had spotted the fleeing poacher and was going down to investigate. Whatever the case, the fact that the aircraft was barely skimming the treetops was surely significant and Sergeant Madikwana knew from experience that this sort of flying often meant excitement and a possible kill. It would be far too dangerous, moving through the jess bush by night but after only a few hours sleep, the sergeant had his men up and ready well before first light. After a hurried meal of tea and dry biscuit, he urged them into action.

All four of his troopers were armed with rifles and grenades while the largest of them carried a heavy machine gun, slung casually over one brawny shoulder. His body was festooned with crossed belts of ammunition.

Madikwana set a brutal pace, but his efforts were rewarded when with the advent of fitful daylight, they picked up the spoor once more.

"The same man:" the sergeant grinned at his companions, "Heavily laden and making for the river, I reckon. With luck, he will have laid up for the night beside the pan and even now, will be sleeping happily, unaware that his life is about to end. Keep your weapons ready and your eyes alert, my warriors and we will make another kill before midday."

Obviously sharing his enthusiasm, the band of fighting policemen checked their weapons and eased heavy, brass rounds into the firing chambers before settling down to an easy run over the last few kilometres to Makorokoro Pan.

They were crack fighting troops and knew that one man on his own had no chance of escape.

***

In the course of a working life that would have killed off most men, Aussie Jack Meadows had known many moments of discomfort, danger and heartfelt anxiety. However, the very first occasion in which he truly panicked came at the moment when he saw the elephant bearing down with such ponderous purpose on his beloved helicopter.

Jack could see exactly what the bull had in mind. The brute would smash up his pride and joy with those terrible tusks and that would mean the end of a lifetimes worth of hope and dreams.

The little chopper wasn't much to show for nearly seven years of dangerous work, but to Jack it was his wealth, his home and his only possession. More than that, the chopper was his friend and had carried him over many thousands of air miles without ever letting him down. It was hardly the fault of that doughty little engine that the pair of them were stuck in a wild forest clearing – himself inside a log palisade and the Gazelle on the point of being smashed to smithereens by a vengeful pachyderm.

For a long, bitter moment, Aussie Jack wondered how he would cope without his helicopter. The machine was insured, but no insurance company was likely to pay out for an aircraft, destroyed by an elephant. They would not believe a word of it. Besides, the Gazelle could not possibly be replaced in the middle of Africa. It had been built in Europe and was the very latest in aeronautical design. Here in the bush, it was literally priceless.

But far more than its monetary value, Jack owed his life to the little machine and the combined genius of the engineers who had built her. Memories raced through his mind and prominent among them was the occasion when they had been caught unawares by a minor cyclone in the eastern highlands of Central Africa. Aussie Jack hadn't seen the storm approaching and the chopper had been thrown about the sky like a scrap of stray flotsam. The controls had been spongy and unresponsive in his hands while the machine wallowed and plunged to every vagary of the howling wind. Joined together in spirit and by Jack's frantic grip on the control column, man and machine had been flung about the boiling clouds and together they had fallen through hundreds of metres, only to be picked up again and catapulted into the heavens.

Jack had stared death in the face that day and even his mocking laughter had done nothing to ease the yawning sense of fatalistic resignation, rising in his belly. On the third gigantic plunge, he saw hard earth rushing up to meet him and braced himself for the crash. This time, he knew he was going to die.

Death is always an occupational hazard to men like Aussie Jack Meadows, but he fought to the very last second to avoid it. He did not want to die and with less than ten metres of turbulent air between the helicopter and unyielding rock, the controls came to life in his hand as the little aircraft joined in the fight. Together they soared out of the storm and together, they laughingly survived to face whatever new dangers the future might throw them into.

There had been other similar incidents and Jack had lost count of the occasions when he and his helicopter had been in mortal danger. They had come through them all relatively unscathed and now in her moment of greatest peril, Jack knew that he could not leave the helpless machine to face the angry elephant on her own.

With a raucous yell of challenge, Aussie Jack Meadows vaulted the log palisade and ran toward the great bull elephant.

***

For many years afterwards, Jason Willard would dine out on his account of the next few minutes.

"If I hadn't seen it myself, I would not have believed it," was his usual comment and his description of the confrontation between wild bull elephant and equally wild Australian pilot was certainly a difficult one to swallow.

After leaving camp well ahead of the helicopter, Willard had driven fast and with almost maniacal skill. Upset and angry with himself, the warden drove with tight lips and his eyes flickering almost unconsciously over the muddy road ahead.

Although the heavy vehicle skidded and slipped alarmingly in places, Willard barely decreased his speed through the more difficult spots and it was not until the sun was well above the horizon that he bogged down for the first time. It was his own fault too. Out of one corner of his eye, he had spotted a herd of stately sable antelope and automatically swivelled his head for a quick look. The Land Rover bounced heavily against a rain gully across the road and the steering wheel spun violently through Willard's fingers. Swearing softly to himself, he quickly steadied the wheel but it was too late. The truck lurched violently then came to a soggy halt, two wheels covered almost to the axles in sticky red mud.

"Bloody hell, Rogers, this we do not need. Cut some branches man and let's get this ruddy rattletrap mobile again."

While game scout, Rogers Makamure piled foliage beneath the wheels, Willard looked around for a suitable anchor for the winch cable. Stretching it to its utmost, he was just able to hook it around the trunk of a stout Mopani tree and was climbing back into the cab when Makamure held up an urgent hand.

"Wait, Sir – listen."

Somewhat impatiently, the warden paused with one leg inside the cab and the other still resting in gooey mud. Doves called contentedly in the trees, but otherwise the bush was silent and Willard shook his head impatiently.

"What are you burbling on about, Man? I can't hear any…."

His voice tailed away as he heard what had alarmed the game scout. Through the heavy silence, the sound of distant shouting was distinct and alarming. There could be no mistaking the sound of a human voice and Willard stood up on the floor of the cab in efforts to see what was happening. Since leaving Nyamaketi, he had heard nothing over the radio and as far as he was aware, he and Makamure were the only human beings within many square kilometres. Yet the distant voice was undoubtedly human and to add to the confusion, it was overlaid by the angry squealing of an elephant.

"Come on, Man. Let's see what is going on."

Snatching his rifle from the cradle inside the cab, Willard set off at a run, his feet slipping and sliding on the greasy ground and gobbets of mud staining his clothing. The game scout followed anxiously, not clear as to what was going on and wondering what he was letting himself in for.

It was a strange sight indeed that confronted the two Parks officers when they burst into a large clearing. Both men skidded to a slimy halt and for a long, pregnant moment, Warden Jason Willard stood immobile, hardly able to believe the evidence of his own eyes.

Aussie Jack Meadows was hardly an imposing presence at the best of times. Although he was very tall, he was skeletally thin and looked as though he could be blown away by even the lightest of winds. When he was angry however, he presented an image of frightening intensity.

"You leave that ruddy aeroplane be, you great, galoofin' galah," he roared at the astonished elephant. "You knock my Betsy about an' I'll skin you alive and use your ruddy ears for shoe shiners."

Despite the patent impracticality of the threat, the great bull paused in its advance upon the stricken helicopter. Swinging to confront the puny creature that had so suddenly changed from fleeing victim to ranting aggressor, the elephant swung its huge head in perplexity. Ears cracking and eyes narrowed even further, the bull peered down at Aussie Jack Meadows, massive tusks raised above the level of its head, the sun glinting off the creamy curves of ivory. Surprised and bewildered, the great beast rocked on one foreleg, its little pig eyes clouded with indecision.

"G'arn; get away from my machine, you overgrown joey," yelled the irate Australian. "It ain't done nothin' to you, so leave off and crawl back into your hole, willya."

The bull took a hesitant step toward the furious pilot and Jason Willard raised the heavy rifle, his thumb automatically reaching for the safety catch. Another step and the elephant towered above the man like the side of a house. Aussie Jack stood his ground and with only three metres of muddy earth between man and beast, Willard knew that he had to do something.

He did not want to shoot the bull. Willard had spent many lonely hours with this very beast and the thought of killing it appalled him. Nevertheless, it was his duty to protect the Australian from the consequences of his own folly and Willard prepared to fire a warning shot over the animal's head. Perhaps that would scare it away, although he knew in his heart that it wouldn't. This beast was 'Mkulunzou' - the Great Elephant – and he was afraid of nothing. Men had already died beneath his charge and with a sigh of resignation, Jason Willard took up the initial trigger pressure with his finger.

The warden need not have worried about Aussie Jack Meadows. The pilot was not going to let himself be trodden on by any animal – not even one as large and fearsome as the Great Elephant. With another angry yell, the lanky Australian whipped the bush hat from his head and hurled it into the animal's face.

The hat – a sweat-stained, mud-spattered scrap of soggy wet felt – thudded against the forehead of the gigantic beast and left it blinking in startled confusion. Bewildered by the unexpected ferocity of the attack, the elephant raised its trunk once more and made a tiny, whimpering sound in its throat. Upset and confused by Aussie Jack's shouted tirade, the huge bull shook its head again, obviously unsure as to what to do next. The fearsomely aggressive pilot shouted further abuse from a position almost between the elephant's forefeet.

"Gerraway with you, you overgrown ruddy bully. Push off and play with the ruddy guinea birds an' leave my Betsy alone willya. Strewth Sport – I'll have your tail for a bookmark if you don't."

Suddenly tiring of hurling mere invective at the animal, Aussie Jack Meadows resorted to more practical attack. Bending from the waist, he scooped up a handful of mud and hurled it after the hat, to be followed by further palm-sized lumps of the glutinous muck. Each wet missile smacked with soggy discomfort into the wrinkled face and Mkulunzou – the largest living animal in Central Africa – backed hesitantly away from its puny attacker.

"G'arn, get out of it, you pigeon toed ruddy emu."

It was all too much for the Great Elephant. He had no fear of mankind, but he had never encountered a specimen like this one and did not know how to react. With a rumble of bewildered indignation, the bull whirled and disappeared hurriedly into the trees, wet mud still thudding against its enormous rump.

Aussie Jack Meadows turned toward the astonished game warden and his cherubic – if somewhat mud-streaked – face reflected unaccustomed indignation.

"Did you see what that bloody monster was about to do, Warden?" He demanded, "Strewth, but the big oaf wanted to flatten my whirly bird. If he did that, where would we be, I ask you."

Jason Willard shook his head in baffled admiration.

"Mr Meadows, you really are something else again. That particular jumbo has killed more men in his time than you have had eggs for breakfast. You chase him away with a hat and some mud and then have the cheek to complain. I have never seen anything like it."

Mention of the hat reminded the bush pilot of his headgear and he erupted into further anger when he found the muddied scrap of felt floating forlornly in a puddle. In turning to flee, the elephant had trodden the hat deep into the ooze and it looked filthy, bedraggled and sadly out of shape.

Carefully rescuing his headgear, the pilot looked across at Willard and afterwards the big warden would swear that Aussie Jack had tears in his eyes.

"Strewth Warden, will you just look at this?" He implored plaintively. "That overgrown rock rabbit has ruined my hat. I'll have his hide for this, I can tell you."

After expressing further forthright opinion on the vanished elephant in basic and uncomplimentary terms, the Australian did what he could to rid the hat of clinging, red mud and jammed it back on to his head. With his face, arms and clothing liberally bespattered and the bedraggled headgear drooping wetly over his eyes, Aussie Jack Meadows looked a comical sight and anything but the heroic bush pilot he might have seemed in other circumstances. Jason Willard smothered his laughter. There were more important matters to worry about.

"What is the matter with your aircraft?" He demanded, but Aussie Jack shrugged bony shoulders.

"Strewth Warden, I dunno. She went crook on me for no reason at all and I had no choice but to bring her down."

Still wiping mud from his face and clothing, the pilot told the story of his own forced landing.

"I reckon it has to be dirt in your fuel supplies at Nyamaketi," he finished off slowly. "Your lady aviator probably filled up from the same drum as I did."

Willard frowned heavily. The pilot was probably right, but it was too late to worry about that. With the helicopter out of action, their arrival at Makorokoro would be seriously delayed, but he had already made far better progress than he would have thought possible in the circumstances. There seemed little alternative but to press on and drive hard for the pan.

"Come on Jack; we'll leave your chopper here and you can ride with me. With an extra pair of hands to assist, we might yet get to the pan in a couple of hours."

The Australian shook his head and there was a ferocious scowl on his face.

"No chance, Warden. I'm not leaving my little egg beater here to be trompled by that monster jumbo of yours. Strewth, Mate; the brute has already had one go at her and there's no telling what he might get up to with me out of the way."

Willard smiled at the imagery evoked.

"Okay, we can leave Rogers here to watch the chopper," he indicated the silent game scout. "He has a rifle in the truck and can deal with any unwelcome visitors."

Rogers Makamure looked doubtful, but the warden had made up his mind and was obviously thinking aloud.

"I'd better let Jim know what is going on. If we are going to have any more delays, he will have to get those Air Force buggers off their backsides."

Fifteen minutes later, the Land Rover had been winched from the mud, a message had been passed to the ecologist at Nyamaketi and reluctant game scout, Rogers Makamure had been left disconsolately guarding the stricken helicopter.

Looking grimly determined and almost as muddy as his new passenger, Warden Jason Willard shot a quick glance at the Australian, slipped the vehicle into gear and rumbled away along the muddy road to Makorokoro Pan.

CHAPTER NINE
(Infection Sets In)

One enormous danger that threatens any person injured in the wilds of Africa is the threat of infection. Although the bush itself is not dirty or contaminated, microbes, bacilli and assorted toxins thrive in the sultry conditions and an open wound has to be treated immediately or sepsis is almost bound to set in very quickly.

When Tracey Kemp's leg smashed so sickeningly against the instrument panel of her aeroplane, her femur snapped like a dry Mopani stick with the force of the impact. Although the break was a clean one, an end of broken bone forced itself through the flesh around her knee and tore its way through the skin, leaving a jagged wound, which bled slowly but regularly throughout the night. The loss of blood was severe and it left the girl weak and nauseous with reaction. Far more serious however was the poison that spread rapidly through the wound and began to creep insidiously up her thigh.

Experienced as she was in the ways of wild places, Tracey would normally have examined her leg immediately after the accident and done what she could to combat the risk of infection. As it was, pain, fear and confusion had driven all thoughts of basic first aid from her mind. Besides which, her medical pack had been left in the aircraft and there was no way that she could have dragged herself back into the wreckage.

The delay in treatment allowed a variety of germs to establish themselves in her bloodstream and although the hours of fitful sleep eased the pain, they further weakened her defences against infection. By the time full daylight arrived, a variety of toxins had established firm hold on her system.

Conversation with the poacher gradually tailed off into

uneasy silence and she tossed her head from side to side in vain efforts to banish the ever increasing discomfort. Sweat poured down her face and her eyes were clouded and unseeing as she drifted back into unconsciousness.

The poacher remained in place, watching the girl in her pain and wrestling with his own dilemma. Like all inhabitants of the deep bush, he knew all about the dangers of septicaemia and readily recognised the symptoms. The girl was already very sick and if help did not arrive soon, she would die.

It was as simple as that.

As a game ranger, the stricken pilot was his sworn enemy and had the situation been reversed, he had no doubt that she would have arrested him for hunting in the park and probably not cared about his pain. For all that, she had proved friendly and was visibly grateful for his presence.

The poacher was a solitary man and had never known appreciation before. True, his family were always thankful when he produced food for their bellies, but his wives no longer acknowledged his efforts on their behalf and all too often, they scolded him because he had not brought enough for themselves and their children. They did not seem to appreciate the risks he ran and of late, the poacher had found himself bitter and resentful of their attitude.

Those wives of his even wanted him to take a job in town, but he was a man of the lonely places and on his one visit to the city, had felt like a captured leopard in a cage. There were many comforts in town, it was true and he had found himself overawed and amazed by the wonders of modern plumbing and the great buildings to be seen, but he pined for the Nata valley and the wide river beside which he had spent his life.

His wives did not appreciate this, yet when he had

explained his problem to this girl who drove the 'ndege,' she had seemed to understand and her sympathetic smile had brightened his entire day. He could not remember when either of his wives had last smiled at him.

But the girl was becoming weaker as malignancy spread through her system and would undoubtedly die if he left her alone or did nothing. He could see fresh blood staining the leg of her overalls and knew that the wound was still bleeding. That was another bad sign and he moved hesitantly forward to probe her injured leg in search of some reaction.

In spite of the gentle nature of his touch, the girl stirred restlessly in her sleep and murmured words he did not understand. Coming to a decision, he withdrew a heavy knife from beneath his clothing. Although he knew that his ministrations would cause her further pain, something had to be done. The knife was razor sharp and he slit through the overalls, pulling the material apart to examine the wound. What he saw made him purse his lips in dismay.

The plump round knee of the 'ndege' driver was swollen like a tight, hard football. A ragged tear in the smooth flesh oozed blood and yellow poison, while the skin around the wound was purple-black and burning hot to the touch. Thoughtfully, the poacher rocked back on his heels.

He had seen similar wounds in the past. He could remember the occasion when his uncle, Simeon – unarguably the greatest hunter in Africa during his lifetime – had been gored by a buffalo and dragged himself back to the village beyond the river. That too had been a frightening injury to behold. Simeon had lingered close to death for many days, but the poacher himself had eventually cured him with the traditional medicines of his people – medicines that were as old as time itself.

The poacher knew that he could do the same for the injured girl, but he was reluctant to interfere. If the medicine did not work and she died anyway, he would be held responsible and the park warden would spare no effort to catch him. Once caught, he would be hanged in the city as other men had been hanged before him. He wanted only to help the girl, but his assistance might well make matters infinitely worse.

Nevertheless, this driver of the park 'ndege' had been kind and the poacher knew that he had to do something before the rampaging poisons ate up her very spirit. Rising abruptly to his feet, he took a last look at the fitfully sleeping pilot and wondered anew at how pretty she was. Briefly placing a calloused fingertip against her burning cheek, he turned and loped away into the trees.

Tracey Kemp was left on the hot, wet earth while overhead, the sun beat down, draining her tortured body of what little strength it had left.

CHAPTER TEN
(Discovery in the Mud)

"Push, Man: push!"

Willard shouted angrily at the straining Australian, but Aussie Jack's reply was unrepeatable.

They had left the heavy fuel drum with the helicopter in order to give themselves more speed, but without the extra weight on board, the Land Rover was proving ever more difficult to handle. For the third time in half an hour, the big vehicle was up to its axles in the soggy road and as the rear wheels spun in response to the accelerator, slimy lumps of mud were kicked up to spatter against the pilot's face, clothes and body. In a dull monotone, Aussie Jack Meadows expressed colourfully abusive opinions on the mud, the countryside, the Land Rover and Jason Willard. His feet slipped in the mud whenever he pushed and on one occasion, the vehicle suddenly shot from its sticky trap and left Jack face downward in the ooze and not the least bit amused.

In spite of his frustration at the repeated delays and his fears for Tracey, Willard could not help the occasional tight smile at his companion's colourful commentary on their difficulties. Aussie Jack was a tonic for frazzled nerves and whenever the warden remembered the lanky Australian's confrontation with the giant elephant, he chuckled quietly to himself. That had been an impressive performance, even by Jason Willard's high standards.

Centimetre by arduous centimetre, the Land Rover hauled itself free of the mud and the almost unrecognisable bush pilot threw himself wearily into the passenger seat.

"That is definitely my lot, Sport."

Aussie Jack was not happy and made no bones about

expressing his displeasure.

"This particular shoveller is coming out on strike. Strewth Warden, I reckon it is high time that you wallowed in muck for a while. I can drive a Land Rover, you know."

"I'm sure you can," Willard agreed mildly. "But from here on the going is going to get even tougher, I'm afraid. We have a number of steep drifts to get through and many of them are difficult even when it is dry.

'As I know the countryside better than you do, perhaps I ought to carry on with the driving, at least for the moment."

Five minutes later, they were axle deep once more and this time, it took the two men almost forty minutes to free themselves. By nine thirty when the sun was hot, Willard and Aussie Jack were both covered in drying mud and totally unrecognisable as a senior game warden and an experienced helicopter pilot.

In fact, it was impossible to see at first glance whether they were black or white – even male or female. They had been reduced to mobile pillars of slime and both of them were extremely unhappy.

And they were still ten kilometres from Makorokoro Pan.

*   *   *

The bull ran hard through the trees, ignoring loose branches and the clinging undergrowth that slapped at his legs. Mkulunzou was no longer angry, but his anger had been replaced by a deep sense of anxious uncertainty. He had been chased away by a maniac with mud in his hands and he did not understand what was going on.

Life was becoming very difficult for the Great Elephant and he ran hard toward the one place in the world where he knew he would be safe. His destination was the deep, dark water of Makorokoro Pan and the dense jess bush with which the pan was surrounded.

*   *   *

Back at Nyamaketi, Jim Lewis replaced the radio handset and grinned somewhat uncertainly at the regional warden.

"That is a relief, Sir," he said. "Jason has found the Aussie and they have teamed up. The chopper is okay, but they reckon our fuel supply is probably contaminated and that was the reason for Tracey coming down.

'It fits too. Some of those drums have been here for months and they are seldom checked before being used."

Regional Warden Makwata merely grunted.

"What about the truck with Sibanda and his crew - any news of them?"

The research officer shook his head.

"They managed to get the vehicle going again, but they are waiting for a smaller river to subside before they can make for the Makorokoro. They have had a good look around the mud flats though and there's no sign of the aircraft, so it has to be at the pan."

"More delay," the regional warden growled. "Even the rivers are against us, Mr Lewis."

Lewis laughed shortly.

"It won't take more than an hour or so, Sir. I know that particular stream and although it is prone to flash floods, they never last long. Willie is a capable lad and he will get them through alright."

They lapsed into casual conversation in the course of which, the regional warden made mention of events elsewhere that brought a gleam to Jim Lewis' eye and an immediate lift to his spirits.

Yet even as the ecologist smiled conspiratorially at his

irascible superior through a cloud of swirling pipe smoke, Willie Sibanda was emerging from the Tombekule River and moving directly into further trouble.

*   *   *

Deep in the dark Mopani forest of the Makorokoro, the poacher moved slowly among the trees. It was nearly half an hour before he spotted what he was looking for.

The tree was taller than those around it and the thin trunk jutted toward the sky like a crudely accusing finger. The leaves were a very pale green, diamond-shaped and scattered sparsely over skeletal branches. The poacher fingered the lower ones with a grimly satisfied smile on his face.

Slicing into the trunk with his knife, the man cut away thin lengths of bark and stripped some of the strange leaves from the branches. Removing his shirt, he wrapped the garment around his spoils and hurried back to the spot where he had left the stricken pilot.

Tracey was deeply unconscious and the breath rasped through her throat in thin, laboured snores. Her cheeks were deeply flushed with suffused blood and the poacher could see that even in the short time, he had been away, her condition had deteriorated considerably.

Carefully exposing the damaged knee once more, he noted the vicious red line stretching into her groin and pursed his lips in deep concern. This was a sure sign that the poison was spreading fast and he did not have much time.

Turning aside from the stricken pilot, he concentrated on what he had to do. Spreading the bark and leaves on the ground, he used his knife to pare tiny slivers of bark, at the same time chewing on the tenderest leaves in order to soften them with his saliva. They tasted bitterly revolting and made him feel nauseous, but his own discomfort was now secondary to the welfare of the critically ill girl and he ignored the feeling.

Once the leaves had been thoroughly masticated, the poacher repeated the process with the slivers of bark. The resultant mush, he mixed into a paste with the crushed leaves and applied the mixture to Tracey Kemp's dreadful wound. As he touched her ravaged flesh, the pilot tossed her head in pain and sweat sprayed from her cheeks. Moaning in agonised delirium, she tried to move his hands away, but he ignored her feeble efforts to interfere.

Once the wound was well packed with the vegetable poultice, the poacher ran down to the edge of the pan and dug deep into black clay, scooping handfuls up in his palms. Something white flashed briefly in the sunlight, but he ignored it and went on with what he was doing. His priority was to doctor the girl.

Kneeling on the ground beside her once more, he packed clay around the injured knee, ignoring her pitiful whimpering as he worked. The mud would set into a makeshift bandage, protecting the wound from further microbic infiltration, while the minerals it contained would combine with the other ingredients to lower her temperature and bring about a gradual process of healing.

By the time, he had completed his ministrations, Tracey was deeply unconscious once more and the poacher wandered uncertainly back to the spot where he had collected the medicinal mud. Even as he approached, he could see the white object gleaming and when he picked it up, he whistled in amazed recognition.

His eyes alight with excitement, the poacher turned back to the girl, an urgent question already bubbling on his lips.

But Tracey Kemp was in no condition to answer any questions.

CHAPTER ELEVEN
(Closing in on the Pan)

"Strewth, Warden: it surely can't be much further. We'd have been better off in a friggin' canoe than your ruddy rattletrap on this track."

They had been travelling for nearly twenty minutes without bogging down and Willard was beginning to wonder whether they might even make it right through to the pan. The thought was a good one and his tone was noticeably lighter as he turned to the impatient pilot.

"If we can keep this up, Jack, we could be there in forty minutes or so."

"And then?"

The warden's stubbled face suddenly clouded. What would they find at the pan? Would Tracey be alive? Would she be badly hurt and perhaps terrified after a night on her own in the wild Makorokoro? His heart ached at the unanswered questions.

Willard was enormously proud of Tracey Kemp. She had always exceeded his expectation, even when he urged her to take up flying, paying for her initial lessons himself. He could still remember his feelings of pride when she qualified as a pilot. He had badgered the regional warden to confirm her appointment to the flying officer post at Nyamaketi and she had justified his confidence on many occasions. She was a careful, competent aviator, but she had never experienced serious trouble in the air and he could only wonder how she had coped.

Jim Lewis had told him of Tracey's calm tones as she brought the crippled aircraft down. 'It was as though she was out for a Saturday evening stroll, Jason,' but for all the ecologist's admiring comments, Jason Willard cursed himself yet again for not being present at the time of the accident. He knew Tracey better than anyone else on earth and his voice would surely have been a great comfort to her when she needed it most.

That she would have been scared, he had no doubt. Nobody could avoid fear when facing extreme danger and although Tracey was a very capable pilot, she possessed all the normal fears and apprehensions of any twenty five year old. How she must have longed for her lover's comforting reassurances as she came down. How she must have wondered at his silence.

Willard's eyes reflected his inner pain. He had let Tracey down. She, who had been a major part of his existence for so long had been left to face her moment of greatest danger entirely alone. He, who had loved her with all his heart and owed her so much for the love she returned, had been found wanting at the moment when he had been most urgently needed. Instead of being on hand to offer comfort and hope, he had been wallowing in his own minor problems.

Jason Willard was an acknowledged world expert on the subject of elephants. He had spent his life among the massive animals and studied them, not only on the ground but also in theory and discussion with other experts. On one occasion, he had exposed an organised circle of ivory poaching in a neighbouring park and over the years, his reputation had increased until he had become an internationally renowned figure in the world of conservation.

But that sort of reputation was expensive to live up to. There were conferences abroad and invitations to speak on the ivory problem in London, New York, Tokyo and Copenhagen. Although flights and accommodation were usually laid on, these trips often necessitated considerable personal expense and in spite of his high international profile, Jason Willard was still just a government employee and not very well paid.

As the warden in charge of one of the largest national parks in Africa, Willard earned less than the average city typist, so the expense of living abroad even temporarily, hit him particularly hard. He knew how much Tracey wanted to get married before going back to university and studying for her Masters' degree, but both marriage and the degree course would take a great deal of money. Willard knew that his massive bank overdraft would never stand it - even if the overdraft had been built up on government business.

Beset with his own financial difficulties, Willard had driven into the bush to soothe his mind among the elephants that were his friends. As a result, the most precious person in his life had crashed her aeroplane without his support to sustain her through the last, dark moments. At that stage, his loving comfort would have been what she needed most and he knew it. Even now she was probably lying in pain and trepidation among the dark and dangerous Mopani trees of the Makorokoro. If she was not already dead. At the thought, Jason Willard's face tightened and his eyes were very bleak.

"What's the matter, Sport?" The helicopter pilot's voice was full of concern. "You look pretty crook all of a sudden."

Willard forced a tight smile.

"Just worrying a little about Tracey," he murmured. "I hope she is okay."

"Aw, she'll be alright, Jase, you'll see. Those Pipers are rugged little crates and if she is as good a flyer as you say, she will have put it down in one piece."

Willard smiled his gratitude for the unexpected reassurance.

"She means a lot to you, the girl huh?" Aussie Jack

went on blithely, his expression full of curiosity.

This time, Willard merely nodded without speaking.

"What is she then – girlfriend or what?"

The big man smiled shyly and for the first time since the previous day, there was genuine enthusiasm in his expression. He grinned across at his passenger.

"She is the only woman I have ever really loved, Jack. I've known her for a very long time and she means the whole world to me."

"So why in the name of Kangaroo Bob have you never made an honest woman out of her, Mate? I mean - you live in the same place, you do the same ruddy job even…. She must be as daft as you to spend her life in a God-forsaken place like this. Why haven't you married her, Man?"

Aussie Jack's voice tailed off as he shook his head and Willard looked momentarily thoughtful. The Australian's question had hit too close to home for comfort.

"How on earth do you fit that great long frame of yours into such a tiny helicopter, Jack?"

He asked the question with a twinkle in his eye and after a momentary hesitation, the helicopter pilot laughed aloud.

"Okay, Jason; I get the message. Mind my own ruddy business huh?"

With his eyes on the road, Willard surreptitiously wiped a tear from the corner of his eye and glanced across at his passenger. When he spoke again, his voice was very serious.

"Tracey means the world to me, Jack. Now it seems that I might be losing her and it breaks me up."

Meadows looked thoughtful.

"Strewth, Warden; now I understand why you have got

fleas in your britches over this one. You must be really going through the mill, Man. Why didn't you tell me this before? I mean… I just thought she was a member of your staff and…"

"Would it have made a difference? I thought your concern was with a fellow aviator. Why should my feelings for her make a difference?"

"Well… I dunno… but…"

Aussie Jack Meadows was momentarily tongue tied, but Willard had said enough. He glanced levelly across at the Australian and his voice was very quiet when he spoke.

"Let's just say," and for a moment he faltered, "that finding Tracey alive is very important to me, but I would put the same effort into rescuing her if she was just another member of my staff or the department."

"She'll be okay, Mate, you'll see," Aussie Jack sounded cheerfully optimistic. "I've seen aircraft go down in rougher stuff than this without the pilots even having a headache afterwards."

There was nothing more to say and conversation died away as Willard concentrated on steering the heavy vehicle through the mud. At times, he wiped sweat from his face, leaving thick smears of red goo across his cheeks. Aussie Jack was similarly daubed and the two men were a strange looking combination as they hurried to the rescue of Tracey Kemp.

***

The big sergeant made a silent hand signal to his men and they flattened themselves into the damp ground. The dark waters of Makorokoro Pan showed through the trees ahead and he searched the area carefully with his eyes before rising slowly to his feet.

Sergeant Madikwana knew the pan of old and felt a shiver of apprehension as he swept his gaze across the flat, brown water. This was an area of crocodiles and desolation. This was a place, haunted by the Spirits of dead men. The sergeant was a simple man and whenever he found himself at the pan, he felt afraid. He could not explain the fear, but it was there, enveloping his personality and obscuring his judgement.

On this occasion, Madikwana's vision was impaired by sunshine reflecting off the water and there was nothing immediately apparent on the muddy banks. He turned back to his men.

"We will take the Eastern shoreline." He told them quietly and there was not a man who did not pay strict attention to his words. Like the sergeant, they knew the pan and its gory history was part of Support Unit legend. None of them liked this area, but they were professional fighting men and would carry out their duty. Besides, the prospect of action and a possible kill were attractive and would ensure that they kept their personal fears in check.

"Three hundred metres ahead," the sergeant went on, "there is an inlet and we will check this carefully. It is a good place to camp and our man might well be there."

The patrol moved on, flitting soundlessly through the trees, their eyes wary and their fingers never far from the cold triggers of their rifles.

In fact, the downed aircraft had been in full view of the sergeant, but in spite of his experience, he had not spotted it. He had been looking for the figure of a man, so the half submerged Piper appeared as a large rock and failed to register on his mind. One trooper had recognised the aircraft for what it was, but he was very young and hadn't liked to draw attention to it in case the wreckage had been there a long time and left him looking foolish.

Had the wrecked machine been brought to Sergeant

Madikwana's attention, matters might well have turned out very differently. The task of the patrol would have remained the same, but their approach would probably have been carried out along different lines and would thereby have saved a great deal of trouble all round.

***

Once again, the poacher felt a prickle of apprehension drift around his shoulders. Danger threatened, but he knew not from where. His nervousness increasing by the moment, he stood up and looked carefully through the full three hundred and sixty degrees of the compass. All he saw was water, trees and dense jess bush. High above his head, a gaudily-coloured bateleur eagle wheeled in the heavens, but the poacher paid it scant attention.

Suddenly, he realised what it was that had brought about his apprehension. The bush was silent. The normal noises of the morning - the chittering of insects, the hoarse chorus of frogs, the sound of a thousand birds and the snorting barks of feeding antelope – had ceased and in their place was a deep, premonitory silence.

Glancing anxiously down at the girl, the poacher saw that her eyes were open. Even though they were clouded with pain, she was fully conscious and he raised one finger to his lips in a gesture for silence. Although she did not respond, he could see that she understood and he moved a few metres away from her position in an effort to identify the threat.

Danger lurked nearby and the bush was waiting and watching to see what would develop.

***

Already delayed for over two hours by the flooded river, Willie Sibanda drove impatiently toward Makorokoro

104

Pan. The road was in far worse condition than the one to Tombekule and Willie was travelling fast. In his heart, he knew that he was travelling too fast, but his anxiety for Tracey Kemp outweighed his normal caution and the end result was inevitable and unfortunate.

Sliding around a tight bend in the road, Willie lost control in the slippery mud and the vehicle went into a headlong, four wheel skid, careering helplessly across the road surface until it came to rest with its prow embedded in a particularly large and solid Mopani tree. Steam hissed from the fractured radiator and there was a look of supreme self disgust on Sibanda's face as he turned to his shocked companions.

"Anyone hurt?" He asked briefly and their heads shook in unison. Thankful for their escape, they climbed from the wrecked vehicle and it did not take long to diagnose the damage.

This time there could be no immediate repair. Even Mark Nicholson's considerable expertise was of little value with a broken radiator and the only recourse was to continue on foot and recover the vehicle at a later date. Fortunately, they were in an area of open woodland where the going was easier than it might have been through the jess, but they were still a long way from the pan. After reporting the accident to a bemused Jim Lewis at Nyamaketi, Willie switched off the radio and summed up his options.

"We will make directly for the river," he told his silent companions. "From there, we can cut inland for the pan and with luck, we can be there in three or four hours."

The fact that the helicopter was no longer involved in the rescue made things seem even more urgent to the young ranger and he set a punishing pace as he led his party through the glowering bush.

***

"So, Mr Lewis," the regional warden was heavily sarcastic; "not only do we have one valuable aircraft destroyed in the Makorokoro and an equally valuable helicopter down somewhere else, but we now have a wrecked Land Cruiser as well.

'Surely, you will now agree with my feelings on the suitability of female pilots in the department?"

"I still think you are being unfair, Sir," Lewis answered steadily. "Tracey's problem was hardly of her own making and we don't know as yet that the Piper has been destroyed. Besides, the fact that we have had a succession of accidents is certainly not her fault."

But Philemon Makwata did not appear convinced and his face was gloomy as he waited for reports of further trouble.

Nor were they long in coming. The big, multi-channel radio set in one corner of the office suddenly hummed into life and after a brief conversation, the operator handed his earphones over to the senior man.

When the regional warden returned to his conversation with Jim Lewis, he was distinctly unhappy.

"That was Support Unit headquarters," he muttered bleakly. "One of their patrols is closing in on a single poacher at Makorokoro Pan. They have seen no sign of our aircraft or Miss Kemp and if she has come down anywhere in that area, she is likely to find herself caught up in a gun battle."

"Oh for God's sake, Sir! Can't those silly buggers hold off until we have found her? They should be joining in the hunt for Tracey - not chasing a ruddy poacher. She could be dying out there and we need all the help we can get."

For Jim Lewis the latest news was grimly disheartening. He had been confident that Tracey would have put the Piper down on the pan itself, but if the aircraft wasn't visible to the fighting men, it meant that it had probably come down somewhere else.

But there was nowhere else. If she had not landed on the pan, Tracey Kemp was almost certainly dead.

Although he knew what the information would do to the big man, Lewis had little alternative but to pick up the radio again and call Jason Willard.

***

Willie Sibanda ought to have been enjoying himself. He and his colleagues were walking through open countryside where mighty trees of African ebony grew at regularly spaced intervals and even though they were still some way from their destination, progress was fast and easy. This was not the dark, clinging jess bush of the Makorokoro. This was savannah countryside at its best, a place where animals gambolled and frisked without fear. This was an area where death was an incidental, rather than the everyday routine it had become in the thick bush, where poachers operated with infuriating impunity. Here there was an abundance of wild life feeding on the rich grass and the animals all seemed relaxed and at peace.

The long-striding patrol passed within metres of unconcerned elephants and even the mothers of hairy little calves watched them with only desultory curiosity. Away to their right, ostrich moved in single file behind a row of bushes, their disembodied heads appearing like stately galleons sailing a leafy sea. Graceful impala kicked without malice and made prodigious leaps into the air for no other reason than good-humoured friskiness. Baboons scratched and a warthog family made off at the approach of the Parks men, rumps bouncing and tails as cockily erect as misplaced radio aerials. A stately kudu bull watched their progress without alarm while his harem

107

browsed nearby, their attention on what they were eating and their thoughts far removed from possible danger. They knew that their lord and master was protecting them and felt no fear.

Although Willie saw all these things and appreciated them as part of his wild world, the tranquil beauty of the countryside only served to accentuate his own misery. He had fouled up the rescue operation and damaged a valuable vehicle in the process. Recovering the Land Cruiser would be a costly business and he would spend weeks battling the resultant paperwork. He might even lose his job.

For the moment, his thoughts were concentrated on his own problems and he had forgotten Tracey Kemp and the accident that was the root cause of his predicament. His three companions sensed his despondency and made no effort to speak. The silence of the bush was broken only by the cooing of foraging doves and the labouring breath of four young men who were rushing to the rescue of a colleague.

At one point, game scout Lovemore Kandeke clicked his tongue behind his cheek and pointed to a small copse of trees, forty metres to the right of their line of travel, As three pair of eyes swivelled to see what had caught his attention, a big male leopard dropped soundlessly from a crooked Mopani and loped away into the scrub, aware of the men but in no particular hurry. The cat was an electrifying sight with early morning sunshine highlighting the dark rosettes and imparting a coppery hue to the richly dappled pelt.

In spite of his preoccupation, Sibanda sighed with pleasure. It was not often that one saw the magnificent hunting cats in broad daylight, even in the Nata valley. Feeling that it had to be an omen and that things could only get better, The ranger pushed on through the trees, his step visibly lighter as his misery began to dissipate .

Twenty five metres further on, the scout clicked his tongue again as he pointed to an area where the earth had been churned up on the edge of a Combretum thicket. Followed by his colleagues, Willie moved across to investigate, although he was far too experienced not to know exactly what he was going to find.

The snare had been cunningly laid and deep gouges in the mud showed where the sable had fought against the cruel wire. Gobbets of earth had been kicked up against the foliage, but the end result had been inevitable and the magnificent animal had died, probably in terror and certainly in great pain. Predators had already moved in and the midnight-black carcass had been ripped apart, although the head stood curiously upright against the trunk of a small tree. Great, scimitar horns swept back from the forehead and the wide brown eyes held an expression of ineffable reproach at a world that had allowed this obscenity. Willie Sibanda felt as though they were staring into his soul and gorge rose to his throat.

There was a pale line of anger around the ranger's lips as he pictured the scene that had taken place and identified with the magnificent animal's torment. Kicking viciously at the remains of the tragedy, Sibanda pocketed the thin length of steel wire and turned bitterly toward his companions.

"If it wasn't for Tracey, I'd set up a bloody ambush and nail the bastard," he muttered grimly. "Until now, the poachers who use snares have steered clear of this part of the park for fear of being shot, but if they feel they can get away with it here, nowhere will be safe.

'Come on – let's keep going."

Taking up the trail once more, the parks men ran in silence, their grim expressions reflecting the hatred they all felt for the brutal invaders who were laying waste their beautiful home.

For his part, Sibanda felt a burning desire to kill the man who had laid the snare. Not only that particular man, but anyone engaged in poaching in the park. He had never killed a man before, but if he had seen a poacher at that stage, he would have gunned him down without compunction.

***

Trying to impart his apprehension to the girl, the poacher spoke urgently, but she found it difficult to understand.

"Wait; wait;" she demanded weakly; "speak slowly so that I can follow whatever it is you're trying to tell me."

But the little man was obviously scared and making an ineffective signal to the bewildered pilot, he slipped back into the shelter of his leafy thicket.

Tracey watched him go with a feeling of deep disappointment. She knew that it was illogical, but there was nothing she could do about it. The man had disappeared among the trees and although she guessed that he was still there, she felt suddenly abandoned and alone.

She also felt strangely afraid.

CHAPTER TWELVE
(The Poacher's Dilemma)

By mid morning, the sun was a viciously flaming ball in the sky. All traces of rain had disappeared and intense heat had hardened the slippery mud into jagged ridges of baked clay. The remains of moisture, left by the night was sucked up and the area around Makorokoro Pan became a gigantic cauldron of steaming air.

Elephants and other animals drank hugely to protect themselves against the discomfort that was surely coming. They had known such days in the past and were well aware of their debilitating effects. Without that instinctive knowledge, men were seldom as well prepared.

An exception was Jason Willard. As he steered the unwieldy Land Rover toward the pan, he studied the sky with an anxious expression on his face. Its very paleness was an ominous warning of conditions to come and he pushed the vehicle to its limits in his efforts to reach Tracey in time.

"This one is going to be a stinker, Jack," he muttered with a gesture at the day outside. "I've known these sort of days before and they are crippling, I can tell you. By midday, it will be so hot that you will lose the spit from your mouth."

"Strewth Warden, I'm sweating like a boiled dingo already," the Australian mopped his face with a colourful handkerchief. "I haven't come across heat like this since I was musterin' cattle on the Queensland plains. Strewth, what wouldn't I give for a stubby now."

"A stubby, Jack?" Willard raised his eyebrows. "Do all Australians speak like you or is this some sort of lingo, you've made up yourself?"

The pilot laughed.

"Stubby bottle of grog – beer," he explained briefly. "A common word in good old-fashioned 'Strine,' Jase. You blokes used to have stubbies here, only you called 'em 'dumpies.'"

The warden nodded with a momentary smile, although his eyes never left the road surface ahead. As he steered the land rover around the sticky patches, his heart began to pound with renewed hope. They were making far better progress than he would have thought possible and every kilometre covered meant that they were that much closer to the pan. Perhaps they might yet find Tracey alive and well.

It had seemed an impossible prospect only a short time previously and Willard mentally urged himself to caution. He knew the bush too well and there was still a long way to go. Bracing his shoulders against the sudden excitement, he concentrated on keeping the truck on the road.

***

The lion was also feeling the heat. The great cat lay in sparse yellow grass, completely visible yet so superbly camouflaged that only a very experienced eye would have picked it out.

The steadily rising temperature made the animal fretful and low, mewling growls came continuously from within the cavernous chest. Hunger pangs cramped its stomach and the damaged leg ached abominably. The length of wire still attached to the limb was an additional irritation and there were long periods when the cat's entire body was racked by helpless trembling. As the heat intensified, the huge beast grew ever more restless and a dim red spark of anger became apparent within the topaz eyes.

Flies swarmed around the predator's muzzle, but it ignored their irritating buzzing, the baleful eyes fixed unseeingly on a spot in the middle distance. When one foolishly curious insect moved to investigate a half-healed scab on a powerful shoulder, the lion's head whipped around with terrifying speed. A massive, rasping tongue slapped down on the afflicted spot and the fly died without even getting a taste of the blood it sought so eagerly.

The lion spent a great deal of its time, licking the wound in its leg and its saliva disinfected the area while keeping marauding parasites and toxins at bay. The flesh around the deeply embedded wire was relatively clean, but the lion's rough and ready treatment could do nothing for the hunger that lay like a persistent ache in the depths of its mighty body.

On a hot day in the Nata Valley, particularly in that area known as the Makorokoro, wind is rarely evident. All breezes die away and the land bakes and cracks beneath the intense heat of the relentless sun. On that particular day, things were slightly different. Coming from nowhere, a vagrant wind eddy sprang up close to the water and skipped, zephyr-like and insubstantial through the surrounding countryside. As it filtered through the bush, it collected a miscellany of odours in its wake and these dispersed almost imperceptibly among the trees.

In spite of – or possibly because of – its hunger, the lion's senses were eagerly alert and although the smell of spreading putrefaction would have been undetectable to human nostrils, the cat had no difficulty in recognising it for what it was.

Its stomach cramping agonisingly at the prospect of sustenance, the lion raised its head and sniffed longingly at the suddenly stilled air. The scent had vanished with the wind, but its memory remained and saliva rose among cruel teeth, bubbling through thin, black lips to burst in a fine spray against silken whiskers. The cat growled in torment, but there was nobody close enough to hear the sound.

Rising stiffly to its feet, the massive animal limped back toward Makorokoro Pan and the scene of its earlier humiliation. The prospect of food was enough to banish the memory of the fear it had experienced during the night. Hunger had taken over and injured, old and in poor condition though it was, the lion was suddenly transformed into an enormously dangerous jungle killer, intent on easing its hunger, no matter what obstacles might lie in its path.

***

Willie Sibanda knew that they were not moving fast enough. He set a cruel pace, but they had passed through the ebony woodlands and were working their way through dense, riverine forest. All four of them cursed and sweated with the effort of extricating themselves from clinging acacia thorns and the dreaded wag n bietjie bushes that dug into and cut any exposed skin. They warily skirted areas of soft mud and moved in varying directions to find game trails that might get them into the Makorokoro with greater speed and ease of movement.

It was mid morning and desperately hot before the senior ranger recognised a particular baobab tree and with a grunt of thankful pleasure, he called a halt. His colleagues gathered around him and Mark Nicholson took a long, grateful drink from the water bottle, he carried clipped to his belt.

"If we cut inland from here," Sibanda told them quietly, "we should be able to reach the pan by midday. I know this tree and it is only eight kilometres from the Northern shoreline.

'What do you guys reckon?"

He turned to each of his colleagues in turn and only game scout Dikito Makonese voiced any objection.

"It is rough country between here and the pan. We will need to go hard and we are already very tired. Better we rest here and...."

His voice tailed away at the look in Sibanda's eye. With a gesture of impatience, the ranger cut through his objections.

"There's no time for rest, Man. We have broken the back of the journey now and you'll just have to manage. Tracey needs our help now, not tomorrow ruddy afternoon. By then she will be dead."

There was no further argument and as soon as they had all slaked their thirst, the little party resumed the march, all thoughts of poachers, tiredness and heat forgotten as their minds focussed on whatever waited for them at Makorokoro Pan.

***

Tracey moaned aloud in her distress. Although her leg felt curiously numb, she missed the companionship of the poacher and wondered where he had gone. Something had been bothering the smelly little man and his very uncertainty added to Tracey's sweating discomfort. The sun was high overhead, flies clustered around her face and she had a feeling of deep foreboding in her stomach. The fire had almost died away and she felt suddenly alone, abandoned and very frightened.

It was nearly eighteen hours since she had brought the Piper down on the pan and she was sure that someone ought to have found her by now. Even in the most difficult circumstances, it was only a seven hour drive from Nyamaketi and Tracey wondered restlessly why she had been abandoned by Jason and her colleagues.

Perhaps the big man didn't need her in his life any more. After all, they had been together a long time and he had never shown any sign of wanting to actually marry her. Perhaps he no longer loved her – had grown tired of her even? Why else had he not spoken on the radio, even when she was going down and he must surely have known what a comfort his voice would have been.

Tears of self pity sprang to Tracey's eyes and she sniffed. The park warden was more than life itself to her. Over the previous few years, he had become her main reason for living. His very presence nearby was a major factor in her happiness and whatever she did in her own life was done with Jason Willard in mind. She needed his approval and his love. She wanted him to be proud of her. Now he had abandoned her to her fate in this terrible place.

Perhaps he had another woman on the side and didn't want her any more. Tracey's eyes narrowed at the thought. Jason had been very withdrawn of late and this might possibly be the reason. She had never thought of him as a womaniser, but if he was carrying on with some floozy, there would obviously be no room for Tracey in his life and certainly explain why he did not want to get married.

Shaking her head against her own thoughts, Tracey made an effort to pull herself together. Of course, there wasn't any other woman in Jason's life. He seldom left the park and when he did, he was usually so busy that there would be little time for dalliance.

Moaning in miserable confusion, Tracey shifted her position, momentarily surprised to discover that the lancing pain which normally accompanied such movement was absent. Turning her head to examine the injured limb, her eyes widened when she saw that it was

116

caked in hard, black mud. It had to be the poacher's handiwork and although the repairs looked pretty rudimentary, the pain had definitely gone and for that, she was profoundly thankful to the little man.

Tears welled once more as she thought about the strange little fellow's obvious concern for her welfare. She didn't know where he had gone or why he had so suddenly disappeared, but she was grateful for the comfort he had given when she needed it most. He might be a criminal, but had proved himself a man of conscience and a wonderful person to know.

Yet even he had abandoned her in her moment of need!

At the thought, Tracey cried out aloud and in his shelter, the poacher shivered at the sound. It contained so much heartbreak and despair and he knew in his heart that it was somehow connected to himself. He felt a desperate need to leave his shelter and comfort the dying girl, but the cold breath of danger still flitted over his body and he was both nervous and worried for the safety of them both.

The 'muti' he had applied to the girl's leg would alleviate the pain and might well lead to eventual recovery, but she needed rest, comfort and expert medical attention. Exposed to the hot sun as she was and in ever increasing danger from he knew not what, the pilot could not possibly be assured of survival, let alone full recovery.

He too was in desperate trouble. The danger, he sensed was very real and he had to move soon, even if it meant abandoning the girl to her fate. He shifted uneasily on his haunches. Even though he knew exactly what he had to do, he just could not bring himself to leave so brave a person alone and unprotected. Nor could he go without warning her of the unknown danger that threatened.

Suddenly remembering the ivory figurine, he had found in the mud, the poacher withdrew it from the recesses of his trousers. It shone white in the hot sunshine and he studied the delicate workmanship with a sense of awe. He had seen others exactly like it – had watched Simeon at work with his whittling knife – and wondered whether this particular article might have been lost by the great hunter himself. Turning the figurine to the light, he shook his head at the thought. The little carving was too shiny, too pristine in condition to have been in the mud for long. The girl must have dropped it in her escape from the wrecked 'ndege.' But why would she have such a figurine in her possession?

Suddenly making up his mind, the poacher slipped silently from his shelter and ran back to the prostrate pilot.

***

The bull slowed his headlong pace as he approached the water. He knew from long experience that the pan was a dangerous spot and almost as though it was reminding him of previous nightmares, the exposed nerve in his right tusk sent a sudden jolt of pain through his face. Easing his way cautiously through the tangled mass of thorny vegetation, he searched the air with a desperate trunk, his mind seeking to identify the scents he was picking up.

Easy to detect among the different smells was that of mankind itself. It was the old, familiar scent that he knew so well and it brought to the elephant's mind a confusing mass of contrasting emotions and memories. The memories were of death, of pain and of vengeful fury. Yet as he approached the pan, the bull felt curiously relieved that the human scent, now drifting to his nostrils was that of Jason Willard, a man who he knew from long experience offered no danger to the mighty elephant.

The warden was close at hand. Mkulunzou had no difficulty in recognising his scent and although he was confused and unsure what this meant, the elephant felt curiously comforted by the big man's presence.

CHAPTER THIRTEEN
(Drama at Makorokoro)

The Land Rover had no doors and the lurch as it dropped into a gully propelled Aussie Jack Meadows into the outside air like the cork from a champagne bottle. Fortunately perhaps, he landed in soft mud, but he landed on his face and when he regained his feet, his language was colourful in the extreme. Wiping sticky red muck from his hair and eyes, he turned angrily back to the vehicle.

The Land Rover had sunk its near side front wheel in the gully and the chassis tilted dangerously forward. In the cab, Jason Willard had his head resting on top of the steering wheel while he pounded the dashboard with an impotently clenched fist. He too was swearing in angry frustration and if his language was not quite so picturesque as that of his companion, it was no less heartfelt for the difference.

Biting back his own angry comments, Aussie Jack laughed sardonically, but there was little humour in the sound. The red headed Australian was an airman. His natural environment was the sky, his home among the crags and valleys of the upper atmosphere. On the ground, he felt awkwardly diffident and their slipping, sliding progress on what was said to be a major road had done nothing to make him feel any better about the forests. They looked okay from above, he reflected bitterly. Indeed, they often appeared staggeringly beautiful, but when one was actually in among the trees, the forest was merely a long, lousy voyage of discomfort and sticky unpleasantness.

Wearily, he staggered back to the stricken vehicle and peered at the disconsolate warden.

"Bugger this for a game of skittles, Mate. I suppose

119

you want me to start digging again?"

Willard shook his head.

"No, don't worry, Jack. If I am right, we are probably close enough to make it on foot from here. We can't be more than a couple of kilometres from the water."

"You want me to WALK?"

In spite of the circumstances, the tall pilot's astonished indignation made Willard smile.

"I'm an aviator, Warden, not a ruddy weekend rambler!" Aussie Jack spoke in pained tones. "Strewth, I haven't walked a whole kilometre since I got my first pair of long pants – and that was a fair old time ago, I'm tellin' you."

Willard remained unmoved.

"It won't do you any harm, Jack. Besides, the alternative is another half hour, digging this crate out of the mud and that will delay us even further."

The pilot cast a withering look at the slime-encrusted Land Rover.

"Okay, Sport – you win then. Lead on and I'm right behind you. You're an okay bloke Warden, but if my feet get sore, you're on your own. I'll wait for you under a tree and catch up on my kip in the meantime."

Willard smiled tightly as he reached behind the seat for his rifle and the medical pack. He had taken the pack from Jack's helicopter and hoped that none of it would be needed. He was in the act of slipping the straps across his shoulders when he heard a terrified scream.

It echoed through the silent trees like a banshee wail and contained so much pain and anguish that both men paused in what they were doing and stood momentarily still, completely transfixed with horror. Aussie Jack Meadows looked at the warden with wide, blue eyes and Jason Willard – strong, capable man of action that he was

– found himself rooted to the spot where he stood. He couldn't even think with any semblance of clarity. That single cry seemed to have petrified his brain and he stared at the pilot with his mouth open and his features blank with shock.

"Steeerewth!"

It was Aussie Jack who recovered first. In spite of his acerbic comments about exercise, the tall Australian turned on his heels and set off through the forest at a long-striding run. After a momentary hesitation, Willard followed, his heart beating wildly and his brain churning over the possibilities of the situation.

The scream – that terrified reflection of fear and pain – had sounded very close, but sound carries a long way when the air is still and they might yet need to run a considerable distance.

It had been a cry for help from Tracey – of that he was certain. She was in trouble, probably even in danger. Whatever the case, she needed help urgently. With an angry snarl, Jason Willard ran after the pilot, adrenaline pumping through his body and his heart surging with emotion.

Deep down in his being, the big warden knew that they were going to discover something terrible at Makorokoro Pan.

***

Crouching anxiously beside the unconscious pilot, the poacher wondered what to do. Even as he watched her face, he saw her eyes open and felt his spirits lift at the sudden light of recognition on her features. She might be an enemy, but she was pleased to see him and for that, the skinny little man was profoundly grateful.

Hesitantly, almost shyly, he held out his fist, slowly

opening the fingers to expose the ivory statuette nestling in the centre of his palm. He heard her little grunt of pleasure, recognised the emotion for what it was and felt immensely pleased with his own selflessness.

Reaching out very slowly, Tracey took the figurine from the man's palm. The chain was still attached and even the clasp was unbroken. It must have somehow worked loose during the crash or its immediate aftermath and in her pain and shock, it had taken time for her to notice the loss. With a smile that made the poacher marvel anew at her beauty, Tracey rubbed the little icon fondly against her cheek before fastening it in place once more around her neck. The man watched her intently, a question hovering on his lips.

"Simeon?" He murmured at last and Tracey looked up in surprise.

"Simeon;" she agreed and his seamed face split into a beaming grin. "How do you know of Simeon?"

He followed the gist of her question even if he did not understand the words and his eyes lit up in the joy of memory.

The great hunter had been the uncle of his mother and although he had been an old man when the poacher was but a boy, Simeon had taken the youngster under his wing and imparted much of the knowledge, gained in a lifetime of illegal hunting. This knowledge had stood the poacher in good stead during his own hunting career and many were the occasions when he had cause to be grateful for the lessons of his mentor.

But even though Simeon had been a great hunter – indeed, many still said that he was the greatest hunter in all of Africa – he had also been a craftsman of note, carving statuettes, bracelets and other trinkets from ivory, ebony or green verdite. His walking sticks had become treasured mementoes among visitors to the country and the poacher had watched him at work on many occasions. As a youth, he had often tried to copy the whittling skills of the old man, although his own creations had been but raw imitations of the real thing.

Struggling for words, he tried hard to convey his feelings for Simeon to the stricken pilot. Tracey listened in quiet fascination. Although she had never set eyes on the man, she had heard many tales of the legendary poacher. Both Willard and Jim Lewis often reminisced about his propensity for cunning, his bush craft and his extraordinary hunting skills. Willard had chased after Simeon for years, had almost caught up with him on occasion and had finally witnessed the man's death on the shores of the Makorokoro – the very pan where Tracey now lay injured and alone apart from a distant relative of the notorious poacher.

Acting on a whim, she would never afterwards be able to explain, Tracey unclipped the silver chain from around her neck and handed the little figurine back to the poacher. It was her talisman – her good luck charm; it had been a gift from the person, she loved most and it had kept her safe through the years. The figurine held enormous sentimental value for Tracey Kemp, but she handed it across to this man who was her sworn enemy without hesitation or qualm.

Uncertainty flared in the poacher's eyes and he searched her face intently for ulterior motive. His own face grave, he eventually clapped his palms lightly together, reached out for the ivory carving with both hands and held it to his chest. When he looked up at Tracey, his eyes shone with the depths of his emotion and he had no need to express his gratitude in words. She could see exactly how he felt.

For the poacher, it was almost unbelievable. With his family, he had mourned reports of Simeon's death on the shores of Makorokoro Pan and on his own, he had searched the dark forest for mementoes of the greatest hunter in Africa. All he had found was a lonely grave where, without confirmation from the men of the Parks Department, he could only assume that his mentor and friend lay buried.

Now he had a tangible memory of the great hunter. Now he could accept Simeon's death as a fact and call on the man's spirit to assist him in his own endeavours. Carefully fastening the clasp around his own skinny neck, he adjusted the chain so that the talisman swung in creamy intensity right in the centre of his chest. His eyes beamed gratitude to the girl and hers were suddenly swimming in sympathetic tears as she returned the look.

At that moment, a massive, black-maned lion burst from the trees right behind the poacher's shoulder. It was less than fifteen metres from the couple on the ground and Tracey could clearly see the massive, hunched shoulders, torn and twitching ears and the wispy mane. She could see the tail lashing rhythmically from side to side and saliva dripping from the terrible jaws. She could even see the angry hatred that burned in the wide yellow eyes of the killer cat.

In the hot morning air, Tracey could smell the lion, could almost have touched it and in that moment, she knew that in spite of everything she had been through and survived, she was going to die.

With the thought, Tracey Kemp threw her head back and shrieked her despair to the heavens.

***

As the Great Bull emerged on to the baked mud that surrounded Makorokoro Pan, it continued to search the sultry midday atmosphere for signs of danger.

The scent of the warden had disappeared, but there were other smells even more alien and these the bull did not appreciate.

The scent of man still lingered in the atmosphere and this was embodied in the two figures beneath the solitary mahogany tree. In one case, the scent was strong and rank – the smell of bush animal overlaying the natural scent of the crouching poacher. In the other, the tang of putrefaction was plain and this made the elephant desperately uneasy.

Elephants are herbivorous animals. They feed on vast quantities of vegetation, never touching the flesh of their fellow creatures and shunning all forms of contact with those predatory beasts that do. Violent death in all its forms never fails to rouse in the gentle giants strong feelings of angry revulsion.

The smell emanating from Tracey's leg was not a strong smell, even to the acute senses of the great bull, but it was a smell, born of violence and a smell that told of death. Overlaying this smell was the stink of a hunting cat and it was this that fed the spark of confusion and anger in the elephant's brain until it was a raging fire.

As far as the bull was concerned, all cats were creatures of violence and death, their very existence an affront to the peaceful giants of the elephant world. Trumpeting its terrible fury, the mighty pachyderm launched itself into a charge.

The object of its anger was the attacking lion.

***

His delight in the little gift and his memories of the man who had so influenced his life were what distracted the poacher and allowed the lion to approach without being seen. The little man saw the sudden flare of panic in

Tracey's eyes and leaped to his feet as she screamed.

The scream itself aroused age old instincts of chivalry in the poacher's skinny breast. It was a cry for help, wrenched from the very depths of the stricken pilot's being and as he whirled to face whatever danger threatened, the poacher found his resolve to protect the injured woman overcoming his natural fear of capture or death.

Even as he turned, the spear was held level in the poacher's hand, but the sight of the lion crouching so close to him was almost too much for the little man's resolve. This time, the beast was in deadly earnest and intent on killing – of that there could be no possible doubt. This time, it would not be frightened off by empty threats or gestures of defiance.

Feeling his knees tremble with fearful reaction, the poacher thrust the spear out in front of him and braced his puny body for the coming impact.

The lion emitted small grunting sounds as it inched its way forward and these sounds fuelled the growing terror of the tensely waiting man. He wanted to run, but with an enormous exercise of will, the poacher stood his ground and waited for the huge beast to spring on to the end of his spear. With a bare eight metres of open ground between them, he knew that death was imminent, but before the killing leap took place, both man and crouching predator were distracted by Mkulunzou. The Great Elephant - possessor of the largest living tusks left in Africa - was bearing down upon them and his intention was obvious.

The poacher whirled to face this new danger and the lion slid to a halt, its eyes blazing frustrated hate and its enormous body twisting in mid stride. For two tortured seconds, the opportunity was there for the man to plunge his spear into the great cat's side, but he was watching the elephant and the chance was missed.

**

In spite of his fevered protestations to the warden, Aussie Jack Meadows was an extremely fit young man and he made faster progress through the trees than his heavily laden companion. In fact, he burst out on the edge of Makorokoro Pan a good twenty seconds before Jason Willard.

"Steeerewth!"

For once in his life, Aussie Jack could find no words, colourful enough to express his feelings at the scene before him. It seemed totally unbelievable.

A girl with the face of an angel and the green overalls of a Parks Department pilot lay prostrate in the mud beneath a huge, leafy tree. Ten metres beyond her, a massive lion spat fury at the very same elephant that had so recently menaced his beloved helicopter and a little to one side, stood a wizened little man in clothing that had definitely seen better days.

Aussie Jack shook his head violently, almost as though to clear it of such impossible visions. Automatically checking his watch, he held it to his ear, this time in pure amazement. It was almost exactly two hours since the helicopter had gone down and they had covered a considerable distance since then, but this was definitely the same elephant. There could be no mistaking its size and the rich curves of those tusks.

Feeling distinctly bemused, the airman turned his attention back to the people on the mud. They were more believable than the elephant, albeit only just.

The little man held a spear, no more robust than the average toothpick and it looked as though he intended to take on both the lion and the charging elephant. Aussie

Jack shook his head yet again. That was surely a messy way to commit suicide. Nobody in their right mind would tangle with a picnicking jackrabbit while armed with a spear like that.

Even as he watched, both the elephant and the little man ran at the lion from different directions. The pachyderm was grimly silent, but the man was shouting in some strange dialect of his own.

Brandishing the spear above his head, he accompanied the elephant in its charge while the beleaguered cat flattened itself into the earth and watched their combined approach. The yellow eyes flickered from one attacker to the other and a thin upper lip curled back in a silent snarl, exposing cruel canines in the process.

The entire scenario took fractions of a second, but with less than five metres between any of the protagonists, the lion lost its nerve. With a rumbling snarl and a defiant flick of its tasselled tail, it spun around and ran in a series of clumsy bounds – straight at Aussie Jack Meadows.

The Australian stood petrified on the edge of the tree line as the gigantic cat hurtled towards him. He wanted to flee, but his legs had turned to jelly and he could only stand still and await his inevitable fate. There was no time for thought, but as he struggled to pull his tangled senses together, Jason Willard ran past him. The warden was panting with exertion and his rifle hung loosely at his side. His eyes were fixed on Tracey Kemp and it was immediately obvious that he had not even seen the charging lion.

It was Tracey's scream, Aussie Jack's warning shout and a gargling snarl that alerted the big man to the terrible danger. The cat had changed direction and was coming for him, blood lust flaming in its eyes. Still running hard, Willard half turned to face the charge, his feet slid out from under him and he fell full length in the slippery mud.

Spray and wet muck flew from the impact and the warden's rifle skidded out of his hand. Scrambling to his knees, he grabbed desperately for the fallen weapon, but even as his fingers closed around the muddy stock, the poacher sprang into action.

The little man had come to the end of his tether. He had spent an uncomfortable night, worrying both for himself and the injured driver of the 'ndege;' he had twice been menaced by the giant killer cat and once by the elephant, he recognised as Mkulunzou. Even now, security force patrols would be closing in on his trail through the bush and to add to his troubles, the park warden had arrived on the scene together with a strange man who seemed to be as tall as any two men ought to be. It was just too much for any man to bear.

With a shout of almost elemental despair and fury, the poacher launched his spear. The petrified Australian watched the weapon spinning in its flight and in spite of his own fear and the dangerous confusion that surrounded him, could not help marvelling at the strength and skill of the little man's throw.

The spear was a light one, but superbly balanced and ideal for use against small antelope. It had never been designed for self defence or hunting lion. Nevertheless, it was kept razor sharp and the blade sliced deep into the massive cat's side.

The lion snarled at the searing pain and whirled in mid spring to break off the spear haft with mighty teeth. Its intended victim forgotten, the predator ran roaring off in a different direction, passing so close to the petrified pilot that Aussie Jack could see the baleful hate in the animal's eyes and smell its acrid stink. As it disappeared into the trees, he shook his head again.

"Strewth!"

Never was the unoriginal comment uttered so

fervently.

***

"Tracey, Tracey; are you okay, my Chicken? Talk to me Sweetheart."

His rifle recovered and his equilibrium restored, Jason Willard had eyes for nothing but the injured girl. The lion was already forgotten and the fact that the poacher had saved his life was dismissed as an irrelevance. Tears streamed down his cheeks as he crouched beside his injured lover. She in turn, looked up at him and her face seemed to light up at his presence.

"I've never had any sheila look at me like that." Aussie Jack Meadows complained to nobody in particular. After looking carefully around to make sure that the lion had definitely gone, he went on in musing tones. "I wonder how it feels."

Wiping mud from his features in a vain effort to pretty himself up, he ambled across to join the warden and Tracey.

Surprised and bewildered at the turn of events, the elephant stood where it had come to a halt and watched the proceedings in complete confusion.

The poacher on the other hand, knew that he had stayed too long. Jason Willard was known as a ruthlessly efficient game warden and he could expect no sympathy from the big man. When the lion charged, there had been a brief moment of hope. With Willard dead or badly mauled, there would have been ample opportunity for escape in the resultant confusion, but in spite of his own predicament, the poacher had thrown his spear and thereby saved the warden's life. With the immediate danger averted and the lion out of the way, a sense of fatalistic acceptance overwhelmed him and he waited numbly for arrest and subsequent incarceration.

But Willard only had eyes for Tracey. Dropping to his knees in the mud, he laid his rifle down beside the girl and took her in his arms, both of them weeping in sniffling communion. It was left to Aussie Jack Meadows to express the gratitude of them all. After a wryly sympathetic glance at the entwined pair, the pilot approached the watching poacher, one hand outstretched and enthusiasm plain on his face.

"Good on yer, Mate," he began fervently. "Strewth, I reckon that was the bravest thing, I've ever seen. I'm Aussie Jack...."

The sound of his voice seemed to galvanise the little man into precipitate action. Without waiting for further introduction, he took to his heels and fled. Crouching low to the mud, he ran for the trees and Willard – belatedly recognising him for what he was – grabbed for his rifle, raising the heavy weapon to his shoulder.

Aiming for the centre of the running man's back, the warden took up the initial trigger pressure and would have shot him dead, had his actions not been stayed by a frantic cry from the girl on the ground.

"Don't shoot him, Jason," her tone was almost hysterical. "Oh please don't shoot him. He is my friend and without him, I would be dead."

Frowning at the words, the warden reluctantly lowered the rifle and turned back to Tracey. Seconds later, his arms were around her again and she sobbed in his embrace while Aussie Jack squatted a little awkwardly beside them.

"I hate to break up the party, Jason," the aviator put in mildly, "but that great, bumbling oaf of an elephant is on his way back and he seems a little less than friendly."

Willard did not appear to hear the warning. He was

totally absorbed in his concern for Tracey and his face was still creased with emotion. Aussie Jack Meadows sighed his acceptance of the situation.

"Okay, I'll sort the big palooka out," he murmured. "I just wish that you folk would remember that I am an airman, not Elephant ruddy Bill. Strewth, man; why must I do all the dirty work?"

With that sad little comment, the pilot stood up to face the steadily advancing behemoth. The bull had initially veered away from the angry lion, its senses confused by the unexpected scenes of utter madness erupting all around it. Standing motionless in the mud, it watched as the cat broke away to charge at the man in the trees and then the advancing warden.

The mighty bull had watched the spear fly and its great body trembled at the memory of similar weapons slicing into its own flesh. Still the elephant remained motionless. It watched Willard approach the girl and recognised the warden as its long term mentor. It saw the poacher run off across the mud and suddenly the Great Elephant had also had enough.

Mkulunzou trusted Jason Willard as much as any wild animal can trust a human being, but the bull had no idea what was going on and the confusion made it angry and upset. Making a deep, rumbling sound in its cavernous chest, the huge beast moved into a shuffling charge, only to be confronted yet again by the strange, mud throwing creature that had already put it to ignominious flight earlier in the day.

Having cast one regretful glance at Jason Willard's rifle, Aussie Jack moved across to face the giant aggressor with far more basic weapons to hand. Hurling further handfuls of wet mud at the six ton behemoth, he yelled feeling abuse at the monster and advanced deliberately towards it.

For Mkulunzou, enough was enough. The elephant had endured more fright and humiliation in one morning than it could ever remember and anger flared in its brain. With a squeal of indignant rage, it bore down on the man and Aussie Jack knew in his heart that he only had one avenue of recourse left to him.

With a sigh of resignation, he removed his hat.

"Gerrof, you stupid, interfering buffoon," the pilot yelled as he hurled his beloved headgear into the elephant's face. "G'arn away and impress your friends in the hills then. I've had enough of you for one day, I can tellya."

With a final, contemptuous 'strewth but you can wear the ruddy thing for all I care,' the pilot turned on his heel and strode back to rejoin the astonished pair under the mahogany tree. Behind him, Mkulunzou touched the offending bush hat with the end of his trunk, whickered uncertainly and walked with battered dignity into the trees.

Open mouthed and unsure of himself, Jason Willard rocked back on his heels and looked hard at his mud-smeared companion. For a moment, the entire situation seemed unreal. He was a practical man, Jason Willard – a man of action and a man who took life by the throat – but everything was moving too fast and he was not sure what was going on.

He had hardly been aware of the lion and was still unsure as to why it had broken off the charge. He had immediately recognised the poacher for what he was and determined at the time to deal with him in due course. When the man took flight, Willard had reacted instinctively.

This was the enemy – the shadowy force that was decimating the more vulnerable park inhabitants and an immediate focus for the big man's pent up frustration and fears for Tracey's safety. He felt not the slightest compunction about killing the man and it was only Tracey's despairing cry that stayed his finger on the trigger, thereby saving the poacher from certain, violent death.

Now it seemed that the poacher was the man who had saved Tracey and Willard looked down at the girl in wondering concern. He noticed the burning cheeks and lines of deep strain around her eyes and knew that she was not out of danger yet. These were clear signs of rampant infection and she had obviously been through a great deal since bringing the aircraft down. Willard felt a deep sense of relief that at last, he was in a position to help and perhaps bring Tracey a little bit of comfort. The escaped poacher was no longer a problem and he hardly noticed Aussie Jack's second encounter with Mkulunzou.

"Oh Jason;" Tracey breathed tearfully. "I'm so glad, you're here."

Willard felt his eyes fill with tears and his love for Tracey swelled to bursting point within his chest. Holding her close with both arms, he was aware of her heart beating strongly against his ribs, although the tension of her body told him that she was still in considerable pain.

At his query, Tracey gestured towards her leg and he saw her lip quiver at the memory of raw pain through the long night. Suddenly, she burst into anguished tears of reaction and the big man comforted her clumsily before getting to work.

A little surprised to see the bandage of hardened mud, Willard used his knife to cut it away and kept his face impassive as he saw the damage beneath the coating. Gently removing fragments of leaf and bark, he sniffed at them, then nodded up at Aussie Jack Meadows, apparently none the worse for his second argument with the Great Elephant.

"'Terminaria Africana' – known locally as 'the healing tree,'" he said softly and when the Australian raised his eyebrows, went on to explain. "As far as I know, it only grows in this valley and is often used by locals as a bush medicine. That little guy must have put it on and I have to admit that he has done a damned good job.

'I'll give Tracey a shot before I fix her up with some proper antibiotics."

As he rummaged in the first aid pack for morphine and a needle, Willard grinned at the helicopter pilot.

"You trying to make a habit of frightening off my favourite jumbo, Jack?"

"He wants my hat – he can have my ruddy hat." The Australian muttered and squatted down beside Tracey to hold out his hand.

"Strewth, Miss, but you've led us a dance an' a bit more, I can tellya. When the warden here gets us back to somewhere half comfortable, I reckon you're goin' to owe me a new hat."

Tracey smiled in weak acknowledgement and forty metres away, the Support Unit sergeant levelled his rifle. His target was Aussie Jack Meadows.

CHAPTER FOURTEEN
(Gunfire in the Mud)

The poacher had not intended to run away. Drained of emotion by his second confrontation with the lion, he had been apathetic about his own future and merely stood in silence, waiting to be taken into custody. He was no longer afraid. After all that had happened, he was unlikely to be shot out of hand and although he still worried about his family, he felt a sense of deep relief that for the moment at least, his days of running were over.

So he stood in listless bemusement, watching the warden at work and patiently waiting for him to finish his ministrations on the injured driver of the 'ndege.' While he stood there, the very tall, thin man approached and his gaze was frankly admiring.

Yet even as Aussie Jack Meadows spoke, the poacher was distracted. From the corner of one eye, he spotted a flash of reflected light among the trees, further up the shoreline. It was only momentary and would have meant nothing to the average man, even a man well versed in the ways of the bush veld.

The poacher was not an ordinary man. He was a perennial fugitive, accustomed to remaining alert to every nuance of bush life that might indicate the presence of those who sought his head. He knew that the flash of light had not been a natural phenomenon. There was nothing on any animal or bird to reflect the sunshine and even traces of mica in the ground would emit sustained reflections. This had disappeared as quickly as it had come and could therefore indicate only one thing – the presence of man.

The only other men, likely to be in this remote area of the park were the security forces and the poacher knew that he could expect no mercy from them. They would gun him down whether the warden was present or not. They would not even think about capturing him or throwing him into jail. That would be too much trouble. A bullet in the head was quicker, cheaper and far more decisive.

So it was that the poacher took to his heels and ran for his life. As he fled, the skin between his shoulder blades tightened with expectation of a heavy bullet, but nothing happened and as he threw himself down in the cover of a small Combretum shrub, he wondered if perhaps he had been mistaken. Had he really seen anything? Could it not have been his already overworked imagination? Confused, but still very wary, the wrinkled little man worked his way through the trees toward the spot where he had seen the reflected light.

***

Jason Willard looked levelly at the helicopter pilot and the expression on his face was bleak.

"She needs urgent medical attention, Jack. The leg is badly broken and infection has already set in. I'm not bad at basic first aid, but this needs major repair work."

"Let me take a look."

The pilot's tone was brisk, his usual, faintly mocking manner suddenly absent. Lips tightly pursed, he peered into the wound and noted the tight shiny skin and thin line of infection running up into Tracey's groin.

"Let's have a decko through the medipak." He demanded tersely.

Wordlessly, Willard pushed the pack across and Aussie Jack searched silently through the contents. Extracting bandages, inflatable splints and assorted packets of medicinal powder, he set to work. Forehead wrinkled in concentration, he cleaned and disinfected the wound, then splinted and bandaged the leg into a more comfortable position. While he worked, Tracey shook her head violently from side to side, whimpering aloud with the pain. At one point, she grabbed Aussie Jack's hand, digging her nails into the skin and staring up at him through imploring eyes. The Australian ignored her distress, gently removing his hand from her grasp and seeming not to notice the jagged tears to his own flesh. Willard held Tracey's head on his lap and murmured soothing words to her while he stroked her face.

Through a haze of pain and morphine-induced semi consciousness, Tracey was aware of the two men and knew that they were trying to help. For the first time since the Piper's engine had cut out on her the previous evening, she felt a sense of relief seeping through her system. With Jason Willard and the man with the strange accent on hand to look after her, everything was bound to turn out well. She felt the tiny prick in her arm as Jack injected another vial of morphine and at last, the terrible pain began to drift away. With Willard's strong arms around her and her mind soothed by the drug, Tracey fell asleep, content with her lot and confident that everything was going to be alright.

"All we need now is to get her on to a saline drip and she'll be good as gold 'till we get her into hospital."

Rubbing his hands briskly together, Aussie Jack grinned at the warden who was watching him strangely.

"You are a man of many parts, Jack," Willard said admiringly. "Where did you learn your first aid?"

The Australian shrugged and seemed to slip imperceptibly back into his normal carefree character. The coldly efficient young man who had patched Tracey's leg had gone, to be replaced by Aussie Jack Meadows – a red-headed daredevil, intent on adventure and fun.

"You know the way it is, Warden. I reckon I musta just

picked it up along the way somehow. Strewth, Man; in my line of business accidents happen and in my time, I've patched up everything from bullet wounds to sheep bites on the bum. I even set my own leg once, although that's another story, I reckon."

He changed the subject disarmingly.

"How are we going to get your bonzer little lady out of here, Mate?"

Rising languidly to his feet, he gestured at the sleeping girl and Willard shrugged. He was about to comment when a bullet kicked up mud beside the Australian's feet.

A millisecond later, they heard the shot.

＊＊

The poacher ran fast through the silent trees, his eyes desperately seeking the danger that he knew in his heart was threatening. A colony of arrow marked babblers burst into raucous clamour above his head, but he ignored the sound. The birds were an everyday feature of life in the bush and certainly no indication of danger. Spotting movement ahead, he paused, seeming to melt into the thick trunk of a Leadwood tree.

At first, he could see nothing untoward. Ahead of him were regularly spaced trees and tangled grey jess bush, apparently empty and unthreatening. Yet there had definitely been movement and he strained his eyes to see it again. Giving up at last, he let his breath out in a silent sigh and was about to move out from his sheltering tree when the turn of a head brought the danger frighteningly to life.

Lying on his belly beneath a spreading acacia thorn bush was an armed man. Clad in camouflage overalls and a floppy hat, he lay with his cheek resting comfortably against the stock of an FN rifle. The poacher could not see the man's eyes, but from the way he was lying, had no doubt that he was watching the little group beneath the mahogany tree, further down the shore line.

The group that contained the badly injured and oh-so-beautiful lady driver of the 'ndege.'

Having picked out one man, the poacher had no difficulty in spotting the rest of the patrol. There were five of them – heavily armed policemen with an air of lethal competence about them. Quite why they wanted to shoot down the warden and his companions, the little man could not imagine, but their intentions were clear. Even as he watched, one man, larger than the rest murmured a few words and eased his own rifle up to a powerful shoulder.

Squinting down the long barrel, this man shifted his position to get comfortable and prepared himself for the shot. From where he stood, the poacher could distinctly see one spatulate finger tightening on the trigger. It required but another millimetre of movement and someone – either the warden, the strange man who chased elephants with his hat or the lovely, innocent lady pilot – was going to die.

Unable to bear the prospect, the poacher screamed his fury and leaped out upon the unsuspecting patrol.

***

The roar of the shot was deafening in the sultry silence that surrounded Makorokoro Pan. Mud splattered over Aussie Jack's boot and the bullet tumbled away in a howling ricochet. Jason Willard threw himself bodily over Tracey to protect her with his bulk while Aussie Jack Meadows whirled angrily to face the new danger.

"What in the name of Kelly's ruddy Uncle is going on now?" He roared across the water. "What wall-eyed wombat is trying to knock my ankles off?"

"I don't know who or what it is," Willard commented quietly. "But that was a rifle shot and it was directed at us, so I would suggest a little caution, Jack."

"Caution be ruddy well buggered! Strewth, Mate, nobody shoots at Aussie Jack Meadows for nothing and gets away with it."

Without further ado, the helicopter pilot charged up the muddy beach, no thoughts of personal safety in his mind. After all, what mere man – even if armed with a rifle – could measure up to the awe inspiring presence of the Great Elephant?

Angry and with his self-confidence overflowing, Aussie Jack Meadows was spoiling for a fight.

***

Sergeant Madikwana had been trying to identify the figures on the shoreline through his rifle sights when the poacher's sudden appearance caused his finger to convulse on the trigger. He didn't see where his shot went as the advent of the shrieking apparition had him scrambling to his feet in undignified panic, rational thought forgotten and the rifle left lying in the mud.

Nor was the big sergeant the only one to panic. The Makorokoro was known as a place of Spirits and all five members of the Support Unit patrol were terrified. The demon-like creature did not wait for them to recover their senses. The poacher had acted without thought and finding himself suddenly surrounded by armed soldiery had also given way to blind, unreasoning panic.

To the fighting men of the Support Unit, he appeared as a thin, wild-eyed apparition – an evil spirit of the thick bush perhaps – and a figure to strike terror into the bravest of souls. By the time, Sergeant Madikwana realised that not only was it not a spirit of any sort, but only a poacher, probably driven mad by the rigours of his life as a fugitive, the little man had run straight through the patrol and was fleeing along the edge of the pan. He ran as though the legions of hell were hard on his heels.

"It is but a poacher." Somebody shouted, but the man was in full flight, his body weaving from side to side in frantic efforts to avoid vengeful bullets. The entire patrol burst out of the bushes in pursuit, only to come face to face with yet another strange and almost unidentifiable creature.

"What in the name of the Dingo Queen do you bludgerin' galahs reckon you're doin'?" Aussie Jack roared his angry challenge. "Strewth, Mate, we've got a badly injured sheila on our hands and you ruddy buffoons start shootin' at us."

Madikwana paused uncertainly and his men milled in confusion behind him. The muddied bush pilot stood in their path with his feet apart and his arms akimbo. With his incredible height and blue eyes blazing through the mud on his face, he made a strangely impressive sight and the sergeant was not sure how to proceed. Beyond the bush pilot, he saw the poacher dive behind Jason Willard and the sleeping girl for protection.

Holding up one big hand to calm the furious Australian, Madikwana tried to explain, but his English was not up to the task of competing with Aussie Jack's amazing metaphors. Shrugging wide shoulders, he eventually pushed past the Australian with a gesture and the policemen moved as a group toward the party beneath the mahogany tree.

Warden Jason Willard watched their approach with considerable relief, the shooting forgotten. The saline drips were with Willie Sibanda in the Land Rover, but the Support Unit men would have some of their own as well as more morphine. They could also assist with carrying

Tracey out to safety. The love of his life was going to be safe after all.

Behind Willard, the poacher watched and waited in silent trepidation. For the moment, he was under the warden's protection, but he knew in his heart that he was not yet out of danger. He had seen the look of angry hatred in the police sergeant's eye and knew that the man would kill him without the slightest hesitation.

CHAPTER FIFTEEN
(Confusion at Makorokoro)

Tracey came foggily to the surface of consciousness. The morphine still held her in its comforting embrace and she was only vaguely aware of her surroundings. Men were milling purposefully around her and she heard their deep voices as though from a long way away. She no longer felt any pain and her leg was neatly cocooned in crepe bandage from her upper thigh to well below her knee, but she found it difficult to remember how that had come about.

Tracey's head was pillowed on a canvas knapsack and her body was covered in a rough blanket, so someone had obviously made an effort to keep her as comfortable as possible. Hazy memories of Jason Willard, another man with a strange way of speaking and an enormous elephant drifted through her mind as she struggled to remember what had happened.

Something bumped against her shoulder and she shifted uneasily to escape the pressure. The nudge came again and she turned her head to see what was amiss.

With his eyes fixed on Tracey's face, the poacher had seen her eyes open and although they were initially devoid of expression or understanding, he watched anxiously as she slowly came to her senses. When he felt that she was properly awake, he nudged her gently. He did not want to draw attention to himself, so the movement was surreptitious and furtive.

Tracey did not respond at first, so he tried again. He needed the pilot's assistance if he was to escape and he needed it urgently. She had to create some sort of a diversion before the warden handed him over to the police patrol. Once those men of Sergeant Madikwana had him in their power, he would die – he knew that and was afraid. It was time for the girl to save him, just as he had saved her during the long, harrowing hours of darkness.

But it wasn't Tracey who provided the diversion. For the third time in only a few hours, the lion burst from the trees and stood out in the open, its lower jaw sagging in a gaping snarl and blood streaming from one shoulder. Battered and bloody though it was, the cat was still a fearsome sight and the topaz eyes that stared across at the gathering of men were filled with angry contempt. At the moment of its appearance, Willard was arguing with the Support Unit sergeant and at first it was only the poacher who noticed the panting cat. He needed no second opportunity.

Prodding Tracey a good deal more urgently, he caught hold of her arm and gestured toward the watching predator. Her eyes widened in shock as she caught sight of the beast and the little man tightened his grip to prevent her crying out her alarm. Glancing pointedly at a thick copse of trees less than thirty metres away, he struggled to get a message across to the girl and even in her drugged state, Tracey understood immediately what he was trying to ask of her.

With a tremulous smile of farewell, she patted the poacher's hand and turned her face back toward the squabbling men and the menacing animal beyond them. Taking a deep breath to steady her nerves, Tracey screamed again and the terror in the sound was not entirely pretence.

Almost as one, the warden, the helicopter pilot and five armed policemen whirled towards her, their eyes wide and their faces suddenly tense. Rifles leaped into the alert position and in the echoes of Tracey's scream, the sound of safety catches being slipped into the release position was unnaturally loud. Careful not to make any sudden movement, Tracey pointed at the crouching lion.

"Don't shoot, Man," Willard rasped angrily as a heavily built trooper raised his rifle. "This is still parks land and that brute is no danger as yet."

The warden seethed with nervous anger, not only at the trigger-happy policeman, but also at himself for the situation in which he seemed to have become embroiled. The Support Unit patrol wanted the poacher's head and he could sympathise with that, but the little man had sought his protection and as park warden, Willard felt a certain amount of somewhat reluctant responsibility towards him.

After all, this was hardly a dangerous poacher. He carried no rifle and had no obvious patronage from those who would purchase the spoils of his hunting. This was merely a tribesman seeking food in the only way he knew. Besides, he had almost certainly saved Tracey's life with his clumsy ministrations and for that, Jason Willard owed him a great deal.

Willard knew that if the poacher was allowed to go free, he would almost certainly return to poach again and must eventually meet his just deserts in the shape of a security force bullet. On the other hand, he could not bring himself to personally authorise the man's death by handing him over to the patrol. He remembered Tracey's anguish when he had been about to shoot the man himself and unlikely though it seemed, he sensed that some sort of strange relationship had developed between the pretty young ranger and the skinny little man.

Struggling with his personal dilemma, the warden paid wary attention to the lion. The cat was very big – an old male with a regal head and a massive chest. It was hurt and in poor condition however and Willard took note of the dangling wire around one foot and the way, the big beast held itself hunched to one side in order to protect the injured leg. The animal was obviously hungry and he could see strings of saliva dripping from the menacing jaws. This hunger, coupled with the animal's pain would make it doubly dangerous.

With a sense of deep regret at the passing of a noble beast, Jason Willard raised the heavy rifle to his shoulder, but even as he squinted down the barrel, the lion charged.

***

Willie Sibanda felt unutterably weary. Like most rangers in the Parks Department, Willie was young, strong and very fit, but he had been setting a cruel pace through very rough country for nearly four hours and the trek was taking its toll. His mind seething with remorseful anger for his own folly, Willie pushed himself onward but with each succeeding kilometre, the pace was slowing and he felt himself totally drained of energy.

Behind him, his colleagues were similarly spent. They moved in listless single file along a narrow game trail, their rifles loosely held and their shoulders bowed beneath the weight of their packs. The only thing that appeared to be keeping them on the move was the thought that with every step, they were drawing closer to Makorokoro Pan.

The sound of a shot brought all four men to life. The bullet howled away through nearby trees and Sibanda heard it thud into the trunk of an old Mopani. Hurling himself to the ground against further attack, he looked anxiously around for the source of the shot, knowing that his companions would be doing the same.

"How far ahead, Simon?" He called to one of the scouts. After thinking for a moment, the man held up two fingers.

"Perhaps two kays, Boss." He muttered and the ranger only paused for a moment.

"In that case, it was not meant for us and it must have

been coming from right beside the pan. It probably means that Tracey is in trouble, so we had better step it out.

'Come on; let's go."

With a sudden spring in their legs and grim determination apparent on their faces, the four young men hurried on through the forest. None of them knew exactly what lay ahead, but they were all determined to rescue their female colleague if that was at all possible. Tracey Kemp was a firm favourite and each of them would willingly have put his own life on the line for the young pilot.

They were almost within sight of their destination when another shot rang out, the echoes like rolling thunder taking a long time to die away. Flat on his stomach once again, Sibanda could hear the confused murmur of distant voices.

"Come on Fellas. I don't know what is happening up ahead, but I reckon we had better speed it up a little."

In spite of their near exhaustion, the four men were up and running forward almost before he had finished speaking. They were almost sprinting as they approached the pan and Sibanda who was in the lead, was the one who came face to face with the fleeing poacher.

***

In spite of its injuries, the lion covered the ground with terrifying speed. For a moment, Jason Willard was lost in admiration for such majestic power. Giant feet padded almost silently over the ground, gaunt shoulder blades angled above the mighty neck and there was no sign of a limp. The beast had forgotten its pain in the fury of attack. The huge animal came at the group of men at a speed in excess of forty kilometres an hour.

As a veteran game warden, only Willard had the

reflexes and experience to face down the killer cat's charge and it was with Willard that the lion had locked its gaze. The warden looked into deep, yellow pools of hate and for a moment, he was afraid in spite of his experience. This was death on the charge and it was his responsibility to stop it in its tracks.

Almost regretfully, Jason Willard whipped his rifle into one shoulder and fired. It was an easy, relaxed movement, made with the grace of a ballet dancer, but the end result was shockingly violent.

In one tiny fraction of a second, the heavy lead bullet flashed across the rapidly diminishing distance between waiting man and charging beast. Slamming through bone and gristle, it expanded on impact, demolishing the pounding heart and instantly killing the giant cat. The maned head dipped in mid spring, the forelegs collapsed and two hundred and sixty five kilograms of murderous muscle rolled over at the big warden's feet.

Looking down at the sprawled carcass, Willard's eyes were ineffably sad.

"Poor old fellow," he murmured. "You didn't deserve that, did you?"

Only Aussie Jack Meadows was close enough to hear the quietly spoken comment and the look he threw the warden was filled with a sudden new respect.

"Okay, the excitement is over. Let's get on with things." Willard snapped at the Support Unit commander. "I want Miss Kemp carried very carefully to my truck and I'll bring the poacher with me. He can be dealt with by the Court."

The burly policeman looked distinctly disappointed, but he rapped out the necessary instructions to his own men. They turned toward the prostrate girl and it was Aussie Jack who summed up the feelings of them all.

"Well, I'll be shagged with a shonky boomerang," The gangly pilot said with infinite feeling. "I reckon that Court might have to do without our bonzer little poaching fella for a while, Jason. He seems to have taken the gap."

The space beside Tracey where the poacher had been sitting was empty and although her eyes were closed, the park pilot's pretty features sported a gentle smile of triumph.

While they had been watching the lion, the poacher had made good his escape.

CHAPTER SIXTEEN
(Explanations)

The only private ward in the little bush hospital was filled to overflowing with tough looking characters.

Tracey Kemp, the only woman present, lay in a single bed, her leg bandaged and held in traction by a set of complicated weights and pulleys. Her pretty face glowed with rude good health and there was a smile in her eyes as she listened to Aussie Jack Meadows. The pilot sat on one side of her bed, long legs tucked uncomfortably beneath him and his blue eyes twinkling with irrepressible good humour.

Jason Willard perched on the other side of the bed and standing behind him were Jim Lewis, Willie Sibanda and Mark Nicholson, together with two game scouts and the entire Support Unit patrol, their rifles an incongruous sight in the sterile surroundings of a hospital ward.

"Strewth, but you led us a merry dance, Girl," Aussie Jack told Tracey happily. "We were running about like headless joeys out there, while you relaxed by the water with that funny little poaching fella. Willie and the other guys lost a land cruiser in the wet, while I had to put my egg beater down in the bush where she was almost trompled by that big brute of a jumbo. Strewth, but I was terrified that I was gonna lose her."

Grinning broadly, he shook his head at Tracey's unspoken question.

"Nah, Girl, it was okay in the end. We picked her up later and with the fuel tanks sluiced out, she's back on circuit and behavin' like the lovely little lady she has always been. I don't have to use my feet to get me around after all, although there were times out there when even that might have been preferable to the things that were happening to me. That Makorokoro place is not good muti, I can tell you."

"Glad to see that you're learning a proper language at last, Jack."

With a rumbling chuckle that seemed to echo around the room, Jason Willard told the others of Aussie Jack's confrontations with the giant elephant and the damage sustained by the Australian's hat.

"I have never seen the old boy looking quite so confused," he said of Mkulunzou. "He is vastly experienced in the ways of mankind, but he has never met anyone quite like Jack here and I reckon he will take weeks to get over it."

Clapping the Australian fondly on the shoulder, the big warden turned back to Tracey his face suddenly grave.

"Why were you so keen to let that poacher escape, Girl? Dopey you might have been, but you created quite a fuss when Sergeant Madikwana here wanted to go after him."

"He saved my life." She told them simply and when she recounted the tale of the lion in the night to her attentive audience, even the big Support Unit sergeant nodded his approval.

"He was a brave man for one so small," he rumbled slowly. "But when I meet up with him again, I shall shoot him just the same."

He patted his rifle and Tracey glared at him as Willie Sibanda broke into the conversation.

"We were just coming up to the pan," he commented. "We had been running flat out for nearly forty minutes and I was really bushed, I'm telling you. Jason's shot sounded just over the rise, then this skinny little guy dashed out from a patch of thick bush and stood for a moment right in front of me. I don't know who was the more surprised and I could so easily have clobbered him there and then, but something held me back."

In truth, it had been the ivory figurine around the poacher's neck that had distracted the ranger. Immediately recognising the little man for what he was, Sibanda had been raising his rifle to his shoulder and his anger at those who had killed the sable would surely have meant the poacher's death, when the carving flashed white in the sunshine and made him pause in confusion. He knew that little statuette. He had seen it before, but even as he searched his memory, the poacher shot past him and disappeared.

"I don't think I've ever seen anyone move so fast," he went on ruefully. "We were all too damned tired to give chase and just pressed on towards the pan and you lot."

He looked around at his men and they nodded their confirmation of the memory. They had arrived at Makorokoro Pan in time to assist with loading Tracey into the Land Rover and getting the vehicle back on to the road. They had even travelled with the girl, but that was only so that they could dig the truck out of the mud when it bogged down, while Willard and the Australian comforted Tracey whenever the jolting movement made her cry out in pain. It had been a long ride and an uncomfortable one, but they had reached Nyamaketi in one piece at last.

While this had been going on, the Support Unit had mounted guard on Aussie Jack's helicopter and Willie Sibanda had started his typed explanations as to how the Land Cruiser had come to grief.

The chopper was eventually uplifted to Nyamaketi. A new radiator for the Land Cruiser was taken down to the crash site and fitted by Mark Nicholson. Tracey was safely ensconced in the little hospital and experts from the Ministry of Aviation flew in to examine the wrecked Piper.

"You will be pleased to hear that their report exonerates you completely, Tracey, My Dear," Regional Warden Philemon Makwata boomed the good news as he entered the ward, uncomfortably bearing a bunch of wilting daisies. "As we thought, the fault lay with contaminated fuel, both in your own case and that of Mr Meadows."

"Call me Aussie Jack, Warden – everyone else does." The lanky pilot invited, but Makwata ignored the interruption and continued.

"They were also extremely complimentary about your flying skills. One comment I overheard was that there are few pilots who could have come down on the pan in one piece, even during daylight hours. In fact, although it couldn't have been much fun for you, this incident confirms my own high opinions of your capabilities and will do your career no harm at all."

Jim Lewis coughed into his tea and the regional warden spared him a brief scowl. Tracey smiled at Aussie Jack Meadows in the shared camaraderie of those who fly and Jason Willard could not help frowning at the interaction between the two of them. Never a jealous man, Willard's self confidence had taken a knock during Tracey's ordeal and he could not help wondering whether her love for him had survived the traumas of the previous twenty four hours. He shifted uncomfortably on the bed and almost as though she knew what he was thinking, Tracey reached out for his hand and gave it an encouraging squeeze. Big, capable man of action that he was, Warden Jason Willard felt suddenly close to tears.

A bell rang through the corridor to signal the end of visiting hour and as he bent to kiss her cheek, Tracey held the warden back with a gently restraining hand.

"There is one thing I haven't told you, Jason," she said quietly and his eyes dropped to the hand, she held at her throat.

"I gave my lucky figurine to the poacher just before he ran off. It seemed the least I could do."

The big man smiled and kissed her again.

"Don't let it worry you, My Love. It was yours to give and besides, Simeon was one of those craftsmen who knew a good thing when he saw it. He carved dozens of those statuettes and I know exactly where they are hidden.

'I'll get you another one so that you can share something with your funny old poacher."

***

Tracey's eyes opened wide when she limped into the office at Nyamaketi three weeks later. The entire staff had gathered to welcome her back and with them were the regional warden, Aussie Jack Meadows and the fighting men from patrol 'Charlie One Three' of the police Support Unit.

They all sang 'For She's a Jolly Good Fellow' in cheerful disharmony and Philemon Makwata made a short speech of welcome. Beer and wine were produced in quantity and a variety of somewhat tasteless snacks had been prepared for the occasion. Tasting a jaded looking cheese straw, Willard resolved to have words with the Nyamaketi kitchen staff.

At one stage in the proceedings, Tracey was cornered by Jim Lewis.

"You did pretty well there, Girl," the research officer told her quietly. "I will never forget how calm and matter of fact you sounded while you were bringing that crate of yours down. I could never have remained that cool and I was proud of you."

"And Jason?" Tracey asked sadly. "Where was he when I needed him?"

During her time in hospital, that question had bothered Tracey far more than anything else. The park warden had visited her every day and shown his love in so many little ways, but she had never put the question to him and he had always seemed strangely evasive when they talked about the accident.

Lewis smiled encouragingly at her.

"Don't blame Jason, Tracey. You know how he loves to spend time with the jumbo when he is worried. I reckon he just had a lot on his mind and took off for a few hours."

"Yes, but that hardly…."

Their conversation was interrupted by the regional warden standing up to make another speech and Tracey bit off her words. Lewis groaned theatrically and raised bushy eyebrows, which made her laugh, her doubts about Jason momentarily forgotten.

"Gentlemen – and Tracey of course," Philemon Makwata began portentously; "I would like to make a short announcement."

"Let's hope it is short." Lewis murmured and Tracey giggled quietly.

"Firstly," the regional warden was saying, "you will all be very pleased to hear that the elephant cull, scheduled for next month has been cancelled."

Across the room, Jason Willard's broad shoulders slumped in unspoken relief and Tracey's eyes shone as she smiled her own gratitude for the news. But Philemon Makwata was still speaking

"A few months ago," he went on, "I approached Warden Willard with a proposition that had been put to me by our Minister himself. Jason was enthusiastic and when you hear what I have to say, you will see why, but he was worried to death by the implications.

'Let me explain.

'It has been decided by Government," he told his suddenly attentive audience, "to institute study bursaries for particularly promising members of our department. The bursaries cover three years of study at any university of the recipient's choice. All regional wardens have been tasked with supplying names of suitable candidates in their respective commands, but I confess that I could only think of one possible beneficiary and that was our Tracey."

Pausing to let the murmur of appreciation die away, he glanced across at the park warden. Gripping Jim Lewis' arm in her hands, Tracey listened with shining eyes.

"I am sure, Jason won't mind me mentioning this, but he has been a worried man of late and as so often happens in this day and age, his worries are all based on his personal cash flow problems. Like the rest of us, he is a long way from being well paid and as a married man, he was doubtful as to whether he could find the necessary finance for back up resources. Even with tuition fees being paid by the government, there would of course be travel and other incidental expenses to find, as well as the cost of post graduate study and research."

"But…"

Tracey felt a great knot of dismay in her stomach at the news. Jason was married. Why had he never mentioned a wife? Why had he allowed her to think that she was the only person in his life? The regional warden ignored her plaintive interjection.

"Of course, if Tracey was to remain single, the department would meet most such expenses, but as a wife, she becomes her husband's responsibility which of course put our warden in a horrible dilemma."

"But…"

Tracey tried again, but in the hum of conversation that greeted the regional warden's news, only Jim Lewis heard her. He merely patted her shoulder while Makwata continued with his tale.

"I discussed the matter at length with Jason and I know for a fact that he has worried himself sick over all this, but I am pleased to announce that his worries can cease forthwith.

'I don't know how the word got out, but our American friend, Randolph Claymore down at Chimanga has offered to match the government grant, dollar for dollar. That way, Tracey can take up the bursary and Jason can carry on with his efforts to save the jumbo of our world.

"But…"

Tracey tried again with no more luck than before. The regional warden was enjoying himself.

"I get the feeling," he turned to frown at the beaming helicopter pilot, "that Mr Meadows – sorry Aussie Jack – here might have had something to do with Mr Claymore's unexpected generosity. After all, he is a very persuasive fellow, our Jack – as Mkulunzou could probably tell us."

All eyes in the room turned toward the tall pilot, looking smugly composed in one corner of the room, but Philemon Makwata still hadn't finished.

"Anyway, Mr Claymore's gift – and there are no strings attached – will cover all incidental expenses and it has been agreed by the Director of Parks that Miss Kemp should be awarded the bursary without further delay.

'Tracey, My Dear, the choice is yours. You can follow up the qualifications, you already have with a Master's degree at whatever university you choose."

Tracey was lost for words, whatever she had been trying to say entirely forgotten. For her, this was a dream come true, but there was one aspect that still had not been cleared up.

"But I keep trying to tell you all – I am not married, so

there isn't a problem anyway."

She said it firmly and every eye in the room turned toward Jason Willard. After a long pause, the big man flushed and looking strangely shy and uncomfortable, pulled himself away from the wall and walked slowly across to Tracey.

"Will you marry me, My Love?" He asked softly and as her eyes filled with tears, he slipped a small emerald ring on to her finger.

This time, it was 'For they are Jolly Good Fellows' and the clapping lasted nearly five minutes while Tracey Kemp cried happy tears against her new fiancé's broad chest.

***

"We've got a dinkum little uni down in Sydney town," Aussie Jack told Tracey considerably later in the evening. "Three years there and you might even learn the language."

"I've been wanting a word with you, Jack," she told him fiercely. "Just how did you find out about all this anyway?"

Just for a moment, the lanky Australian looked uncomfortable. He glanced quickly across at Jim Lewis, but the ecologist was staring fixedly into the depths of his glass.

"Er... I just sort of heard it, I suppose. It seems pretty obvious that you and the big fella will make a great couple and it seemed a shame that lack of the ready should stick a spanner in the spokes. I sorta mentioned it to Old Man Claymore and kinda went on to hint that he could find himself looking for rhino on foot next year, so there we were. Strewth Trace, he can afford it. He'll probably write the cabbage off against income tax and we all end up

159

chuffed as ruddy pigeons."

"Why should you be so pleased?" Tracey didn't even attempt to understand the strangled metaphor. "What's in it for you, Jack?"

The tall Australian seemed to shrink slightly against the wall.

"Well, nothing really, although I did sort of suggest to Jason that he might need an aviator as his Best Man. You know… someone to handle the…."

Blushing to the roots of his tangled hair, the lanky Australian went on.

"I also sorta mentioned that when my contract with Claymore's outfit comes to an end, you all might need a chopper driver to assist around here. We could fly together during your vacations and I could sort of chauffeur you and…"

He tailed off at the fierce look in his fellow aviator's eye and Tracey looked sternly at him. For once in his life, Aussie Jack Meadows was lost for words.

Tracey looked wordlessly at the tall man for a long moment, then put her arms around his neck and kissed him gently on the cheek.

"You are a treasure, Jack," she told him. "Even if I cannot understand a single word you say."

The helicopter pilot rubbed his cheek with a look of such bemusement in his eye that everyone exploded into laughter. The party continued well into the evening and when it finally wound down, Tracey thanked everyone concerned and with Jason Willard on one side and Aussie Jack on the other, prepared to walk home. With one hand tucked beneath the warden's arm and the other around the Australian's waist, she hobbled from the room to the cheers of the remaining guests.

Outside the moon was almost full and in the middle

distance, a lion coughed throatily to inform the world that he was abroad and looking for love. Nearer at hand, nightjars trilled to each other and Tracey sighed with pleasure at the joys of being back in her own wild world.

"Why didn't you tell me?" She demanded quietly of Jason Willard as they approached his little cottage. "We could have sorted something out and you don't have to marry me, you know."

The big game warden only smiled and pressed her hand against his body. Even through his heavy bush shirt, she could feel the love he felt for her and that, together with the ring on her finger was answer enough.

***

On the veranda wall at Nyamaketi, a newly mounted lion head peered with regal arrogance into the moonlit darkness and across the mighty river, a small, wrinkled man prepared for his next hunting expedition. Bidding his wives and children farewell, he fingered an intricately carved piece of ivory, dangling from his neck and disappeared into the night.

The End

GLOSSARY

CITES: The United Nations Commission For Investigating Trade in Endangered Species.

Comms: Communications.

Combretum: Vegetation of the bushwillow family, of which there are some three hundred varieties in Southern Africa.

Jess: Particularly thick and impenetrable vegetation.

Kalashnikov: Automatic assault rifle, manufactured in Eastern Europe.

Mayday: Internationally recognised distress call. Only used in emergency.

Muti: Medicine.

Ndege: Bird, but applied to aeroplanes through most of Africa.

Nganga: Traditional healer or herbal doctor.

Nyama: Meat.

Pan: Small inland lake or water hole.

PPL: Private Pilot's Licence.

Shumba: Lion.

Skellums: Evil or mischievous things.

Strine: Australian slang language.

Veld: Bush – normally applies to open grassland.

Wag n'bietjie: Literally 'wait a bit' – applies mainly to the Acacia Caffre shrub, which bears cruelly hooked thorns.

And of course there were many words used in this story that only Aussie Jack could explain.

Other books by David Lemon

Ivory Madness: The College Press 1983

Africa's Inland Sea: Modus Press 1987

Kariba Adventure: The College Press 1988

Rhino: Puffin Books 1989

Man Eater: Viking Books 1990

Hobo Rows Kariba: African Publishing Group 1997

Killer Cat: The College Press 1998

Never Quite a Soldier: Albida Books 2000

Never Quite a Soldier (South African edition): Galago
Books 2006

Blood Sweat and Lions: Grosvenor House Publishing
2008

Two Wheels and a Tokoloshe: Grosvenor House
Publishing 2008

Hobo: Grosvenor House Publishing 2009

Soldier No More: Grosvenor House Publishing 2011

Cowbells Down the Zambezi: Grosvenor House
Publishing 2013

Printed in Great Britain
by Amazon